Welcome to the Secret World of Alex Mack!

When my new friend Chris Gordon invited me to ride in one of his dad's glider planes, I jumped at the chance. I have some pretty amazing powers, but one thing I can't do is *fly*. But now someone is trying to sabotage the planes . . . and I'm tempted to use what powers I have to stop him. Let me explain:

I'm Alex Mack. I was just another average kid until my first day of junior high.

One minute I'm walking home from school—the next there's a *crash!* A truck from the Paradise Valley Chemical plant overturns in front of me and I'm drenched in some weird chemical.

And since then—well, nothing's been the same. I can move objects with my mind, shoot electrical charges through my fingertips, and morph into a liquid shape . . . which is handy when I get in a tight spot!

My best friend, Ray, thinks it's cool—and my sister, Annie, thinks I'm a science project.

They're the only two people who know about my new powers. I can't let anyone else find out—not even my parents—because I know the chemical plant wants to find me and turn me into some experiment.

But you know something? I guess I'm not so average anymore!

The Secret World of Alex Mack™

Alex, You're Glowing!
Bet You Can't!
Bad News Babysitting!
Witch Hunt!
Mistaken Identity!
Cleanup Catastrophe!
Take a Hike!
Go for the Gold!
Poison in Paradise!
Super Edition: Zappy Holidays!
Junkyard Jitters!
Frozen Stiff!
I Spy!
High Flyer!

Available from MINSTREL Books

High Flyer!

Patricia Barnes-Svarney

Published by POCKET BOOKS
New York London Toronto Sydney Tokyo Singapore

A MINSTREL PAPERBACK *Original*

A Minstrel Book published by
POCKET BOOKS, a division of Simon & Schuster Inc.
1230 Avenue of the Americas, New York, NY 10020

ISBN: 0-671-00449-2

First Minstrel Books printing April 1997

10 9 8 7 6 5 4 3 2 1

Front cover photo by Pat Hill Studio

Printed in the U.S.A.

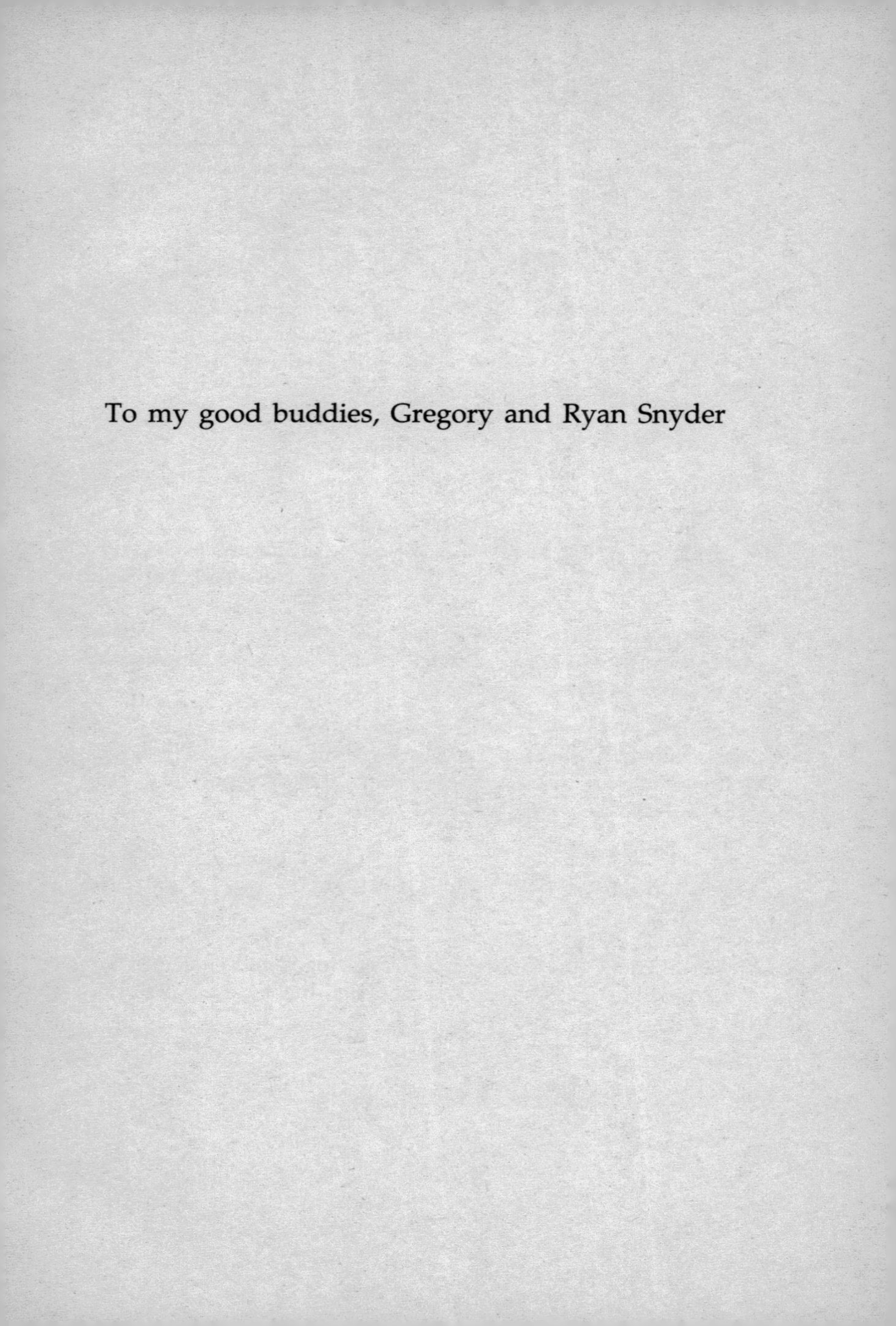

To my good buddies, Gregory and Ryan Snyder

High Flyer!

CHAPTER 1

"Ready?" Robyn Russo asked.

"Check," Alex said, her arm in position.

"Set?"

"Check."

"Go!"

Alex Mack tossed the small paper airplane past her good friend Robyn. The paper flyer circled once, cleared Robyn's nose by a fraction of an inch, then made a maddening spiral to the ground—just like the last paper airplane. As it landed at her feet, Robyn shook her head.

"Another bomb, Alex. What a bummer."

Alex stared at the crushed, blue folded paper on the floor and nodded. "A total flop."

"This is just great," said Robyn, plopping down on her chair. "We're probably the only ninth graders in the history of science who can't get a paper airplane to fly more than two feet. Usually the teachers don't want us to throw paper airplanes. Now, when we finally get permission to, we can barely get the thing off the ground."

"Don't worry, Robyn. We'll figure something out," Alex said. "Remember what Mrs. Dellia told us? All the great inventors had to go through trial and error. We learn through our mistakes, right?"

Robyn didn't look convinced. And Alex understood how she felt. It seemed as if every time she and Robyn tried to solve their latest science experiment, the laws of the universe were against them. And as usual, when things went wrong in science lab, Alex thought about her sister, Annie, the science brain of the family. Annie would think the airplane project was child's play. Alex wished Annie would materialize out of thin air and tell them how to solve their latest problem.

But deep down inside, Alex was beginning to enjoy seeking the answers to her science problems herself. *Annie doesn't have to be the only mad scientist in the family,* Alex thought. *I could have inherited a few of those brainiac genes from Dad, too.* Alex was hoping to boost her science grade even higher than last semester by doing well on the paper airplane project.

"All right," said Alex. She rolled up the sleeves of her red plaid blouse and pulled out her spiral notebook. "First, that construction paper may be too heavy. So let's use lighter paper from my notebook. That may work better."

Robyn scowled and rested her head in her right hand, her long red hair escaping from its bun. "Lighter paper. Right. Maybe we should use feathers. Birds have feathers and they fly. But then, where would we get the feathers? I certainly don't want to get them from a bird. Gross."

Alex sighed. Sometimes she regretted having Robyn for a lab partner. She viewed everything as a worst-case scenario and never seemed to see the good in any situation. But then again, she was one of Alex's best friends—and she wasn't *always* that negative.

"Come on, Robyn. Snap out of it," Alex urged. "We can do this." She tore a piece of plain paper from her lab notebook and started to fold it along two edges, forming the nose of the plane. Turning the paper over carefully, she bent the sides to create two sleek wings. "Think rudder, Robyn. The lab sheet says we need a rudder," Alex said, still concentrating on the airplane.

As she grabbed a nearby roll of tape, a voice came from across the room. "Check it out, Alex, if you want to see a technological masterpiece in action." Alex looked up and saw Raymond Alvarado holding a strange-looking yellow and green paper airplane. Ray was Alex's best friend, and besides Annie, the only person who knew about her secret powers. *Knowing Ray, he's wondering why I don't just use my powers to make my airplane fly,* she thought.

Ray let his airplane fly. It glided smoothly across the room, directly into the outstretched hand of his partner, Louis Driscoll.

Ray looked very proud of himself. Alex congratulated him and turned back to her plane. She continued to tape the flyer together, keeping track of the lab directions as she worked.

"We call it the Wondersonic Space Shuttle," Ray said, catching the plane that Louis had sent back to him.

Robyn scrunched her face. "More like the 'Wonder-If-It-Will-Crash Space Shuttle.' "

Ray looked hurt as he turned to his lab partner, Louis. "Hey, that sounds like sour grapes to me. How about you, Mr. Louis 'Orville' Driscoll?"

"Agreed, Mr. Raymond 'Wilbur' Alvarado," said Louis, a lock of his reddish brown hair falling onto his forehead. "Great genius is never recognized in its own time."

Alex rolled her eyes and returned to her airplane.

Louis sat down and started spinning on his lab stool. "Let us know if you'd like to use us as consultants," he generously offered Alex and Robyn. "We'd be happy to share our expertise in plane—"

"Not a plane, a Wondersonic Space Shuttle," Ray corrected.

"Oh, yeah, right," Louis said. "Anyway, we found this great software program on my dad's computer that prints out paper airplanes. It even gives directions on how to fold the things."

"Ah, ha!" Robyn exclaimed. "I knew it."

"But I still knew how to do it intuitively," Ray said. "After all, I'm going to become a pilot some day."

"Of course," Robyn said, nudging Alex with her elbow. "And does this mean you don't want to be an ornithologist anymore?"

Alex chuckled. Every week, Ray came up with another career he wanted to try, and each week he swore that it was *the* one. His latest idea was to be like Roger Tory Peterson—the ornithologist they'd learned about in science class last week—and study the behavior of birds.

"That was last week," Louis added helpfully. "Now he's into flying himself instead of watching birds fly."

Alex snickered. "How about you, 'Orville'? Are you going to be Ray's copilot?"

"Yeah. Sure. Flying. I love it." Louis tried, but failed, to smile. He stopped spinning on his stool and opened a nearby notebook. Alex thought he looked a little gray all of a sudden. He didn't seem to like the idea of flying as much as he let on.

"So, anyone for a contest?" asked Ray, holding the paper airplane high in the air and making jet noises in his throat.

"Excuse me?"

Ray turned around. Mrs. Dellia was standing right behind him, her arms crossed in front of her and a stern look on her face. "Or . . . maybe . . . I'll just sit down," Ray added, reaching out for his stool and sitting down quickly.

"Thank you, Mr. Alvarado," said Mrs. Dellia. "I was going to suggest that you do just that. And I think you should let Alex and Robyn concentrate on their own project." She walked over to Alex and looked over her shoulder. "So how is it going? Did you figure out a design?"

Alex liked Mrs. Dellia. "We've got a design—sort of," Alex said. "We thought it would work, but we think the paper was too heavy." Alex held up a drawing she and Robyn developed the night before with the help of Alex's father. At first, she and Robyn wanted Annie to help them with the design, but it was the night her sister tutored a girl down the street in math. Mr. Mack didn't seem to mind helping them with the lab project: He was a chemist at Paradise Valley Chemical Plant and loved anything to do with science.

Mrs. Dellia frowned. "What's that sticking up from the back of your plane?" she asked, pointing to the drawing.

"That's my idea, Mrs. Dellia," Robyn said proudly. "It's a lightning rod."

"A lightning rod," the teacher repeated slowly.

"Yeah. In case of bad weather."

Alex concentrated harder on the paper flyer, trying not to look at Mrs. Dellia. It was Robyn's idea to put on the lightning rod. In fact, Robyn wanted to add more features based on all the worst-case scenarios she could think of—meteorite showers, gigantic flying birds, that sort of thing—but Alex had talked her out of most of them.

Mrs. Dellia cleared her throat. "Okay, girls, continue on. I'll be very interested in seeing your results." She turned around and headed for the next lab table.

"Need help?"

Alex looked up to see Chris Gordon standing in front of her. He was a tall, brown-haired student who had moved to Paradise Valley only about a year ago. Alex didn't know him very well, except that he was one of the top math students in the school. And until about a month ago, when she sat next to him at a school band concert, she had really never paid much attention to him. After that, she often saw him in the school halls and they would smile and wave to each other. One time, he even stopped at her locker to ask her how she did on the latest science test.

"Chris! Hi! Yeah, we could use some help," Robyn said, reaching for the drawing of their airplane.

Alex kicked Robyn under the lab table. "That's okay, Chris. We're doing fine," Alex said. She didn't want to look like a dufus in front of Chris. Plus, she wanted to figure out what the problem was with her plane on her own.

"I was just watching you both from across the room," Chris continued. "Your design is fine. But you have to learn why the plane flies through the air."

"They probably need more jet fuel," Louis joked from across the aisle.

Chris smiled at Louis, then turned to Alex and

Robyn again. "It's based on the physics of lift," Chris explained, holding up Alex's pencil to demonstrate. "It's the force that offsets the airplane's weight. It depends on the shape of the plane, the airspeed, the shape and size of the wing, and the air density. And of course, it depends on how you throw the paper airplane—or launch your wonder-plane," he added, looking over at Ray.

"Shuttle, please," said Ray, folding his arms over his chest.

"You mean all we have to do is understand lift?" Alex asked.

Chris turned back to Alex. "Not really. But for now, I think lift is the most useful force."

"And how did you get so smart?" asked Louis.

"I've been flying since I was seven years old," Chris said. He gave the pencil back to Alex. "I've even piloted some small planes and gliders."

Louis shrugged and began to spin on his stool again.

"Gliders? Those are the planes without engines, right?" asked Alex.

"Yeah. They're called gliders or sailplanes,'' said Chris. He looked out the window and into the sky. ''Flying in them makes you feel like you're soaring like an eagle.''

''Where do you fly?'' she asked.

''Mostly at Windsock Field. There's a gliderport there.''

Alex frowned. ''Windsock? Isn't that the airfield near the Paradise Valley Chemical Plant?''

''Yeah, that's the one,'' Chris said.

Alex suddenly shivered. Saying ''Paradise Valley Chemical Plant'' definitely made her jumpy. It reminded her of the crazy powers she'd developed after being doused with the chemical GC-161 during an accident with a PVC truck. Lately, she seemed to be controlling her powers much better—at least she hoped so.

''And you, Alex?''

Alex snapped out of her thoughts and looked up at Chris. ''Me what?''

''Did your shuttle take off already, space cadet?'' Ray joked.

Robyn put her hand under her chin and stared up at Chris. Alex wanted to kick her again to stop her from staring, but Robyn had moved away and closer to Chris. Alex knew Robyn thought he was cute, but Alex just liked him as a friend. Looking up at Chris, she had to admit silently that he was pretty cute.

"Well, I think it's great, Chris," Robyn was saying. "Unpowered flight. Gliding sounds very, well . . . adventurous. Make that dangerous . . . but adventurous."

"Class! Time to call it quits," Mrs. Dellia said, standing in the front of the lab tables. "Some of you aren't quite finished yet, so I'm giving you all until next week. Let's see if you can come up with some really great details for your airplanes. Class dismissed."

Chris turned and walked back to his desk to gather his backpack. Robyn sighed and leaned toward Alex. "Isn't he cute?" she whispered.

Alex smiled and nodded, grabbed her notebook, and headed out the door. She and Robyn said goodbye, and Alex walked quickly down the hall to her locker. As she spun the lock, she tried to remember her new combination. Six . . . Twelve . . . Nine . . . *I wish we'd keep the same locker combinations every semester,* she thought. *Now, was the last number six or ten? Then again, why don't I just send out a zapper and—*

"Don't you hate it when they give us new locker combinations?"

Alex jumped. She turned to see Chris Gordon leaning on the locker next to hers.

"Chris! Oh, yeah, really. It drives me crazy," she said, finally remembering the last number and opening the lock. "By the way, thanks for helping Robyn and me back there."

"Sure. No problem. I just wondered. You seemed really interested in gliding. There's this thing called 'Open House Saturday' at Windsock Field. Some of the people at the gliderport give free rides that day—but only to invited people. I was wondering if you'd like to go," he said, then hesitated. "You can ask your parents to come along, and anyone else. Maybe Robyn, even Ray and Louis."

"Ummm . . . great," she said, dragging some books out of the locker and tucking them into her left arm. She hesitated before saying anything else. She hadn't really thought about gliding in a *real* plane. She once rode in a commercial airplane when she visited her grandmother in Florida. But she didn't really remember too much—she was only six years old at the time. "Listen. Chris," she said, closing her locker. "I'll have to ask my parents. I'll give you a call."

"Okay. My number's in the phone book under Bud Gordon on Grant Street," he said. "Later!"

Alex smiled as she watched Chris walk toward his next class. Gliding could be fun. Chris said it felt like you were soaring like an eagle. Now that's *one* power she didn't have.

CHAPTER 2

"Soaring? At the gliderport?"

Sitting across from her mother at the dining room table, Alex watched her face. Alex hoped that a satisfying, filling meal might help her parents say yes about going to the gliderport. She had also helped set the table, cleaned the stove after Mrs. Mack had spilled the corn, and volunteered to wash and dry the dishes that night.

"Chris Gordon asked me. Well, he really asked me to ask everyone if they wanted to go," Alex tried to explain.

"Now I know why you've been so helpful all evening, Alex," said Annie, reaching over for the pepper shaker. "You're trying to soften up Mom and Dad."

"I don't know, Alex," said her mother, looking over at Mr. Mack. "It sounds—"

"Great!" Mr. Mack finished. He bit into a piece of bread and smiled as he chewed.

Mrs. Mack frowned. "I don't know, George. Do you think—"

"Listen, Barbara," he said, swallowing. "Remember that paper you have to write for your English class? And remember how you've been driving us crazy all week, trying to come up with something to write about?"

"It's not English class, George. It's creative writing class." Alex's mother had recently decided to go back to college to get her master's degree. Mrs. Mack would often mention how she felt bad that she was ignoring the family. But Alex didn't mind when her mother had to study. It was good that she was doing something that she really wanted to do—and she seemed happier ever since she started school.

"Yeah, Mom," added Alex, picking up on her father's idea. "You can write about soaring in a glider!"

Mrs. Mack toyed with her fork. "Well, I—"

"I can picture it now," said Annie, squinting her eyes. "The title: 'Giddy in a Glider.' "

"Or how about 'High Flyer'?" Alex suggested.

"Hmmm . . . I like that, Alex," said Mrs. Mack, cocking her head.

"Sounds like a hit motion picture to me," Mr. Mack added, winking at his wife.

"Oh . . ." Mrs. Mack said, hesitating. "Oh, all right. It sounds like a great idea to me, too." Turning to Alex, she asked, "When do we go?"

"It's being held this weekend—Saturday." Alex answered. She was sure her mother would have something else planned. Since she started back at college, she usually studied or caught up on chores around the house on weekends.

But her mother surprised her. "Wonderful," Mrs. Mack said, clapping her hands together. "I don't have any homework this weekend, except for the creative writing paper. So it will work out perfectly."

Saturday turned out to be a bright, sunny day. The winds were calm, and the temperature was so warm that Alex only needed to wear a light yellow T-shirt and cut-off blue jeans to the air-field. She had called her friends after dinner on Wednesday and everyone but Nicole—she had to go to a recital—had agreed to go. So after Saturday's lunch, Alex, Mr. and Mrs. Mack, Annie, Robyn, Louis, and Ray were all packed like sardines in the Macks' family car and on their way to Windsock Field.

Everyone was excited at the prospect of going gliding. The only one who had needed some convincing was Louis. When she'd called him, he said he had to go to his aunt's house for a family picnic. Alex thought that was strange. Usually, Louis would do anything to get out of going to a family picnic—and seeing his obnoxious twin cousins, Rodney and Randy. When she reminded him of this, he hesitated, then agreed to go. But she didn't think he sounded too excited about it.

The gliderport was a flat field set on the top of a steep hill. It almost looked as though a giant had sliced off the top of the hill so people could build the airport there. As Alex gazed out the car window, she could see four planes sitting along the sides of the field's grassy runway.

"There's one flying now!" Ray exclaimed. He pointed to the sky as he jumped out of the car.

Everyone looked up. There, soaring in the light breeze, was a bright orange sailplane. Shading her eyes, Alex watched as the quiet glider flew over the trees surrounding the far side of the field and made a gentle landing on the freshly mowed runway.

"Oh, great!" said Robyn, turning and reaching back into the car.

"What's wrong?" asked Alex, leaning into the car. Robyn was digging through her large brown purse.

"My camera. I brought it with me. I really don't want to fly. I just want to take pictures of the gliders—and of you guys flying, of course. I'm hoping I can give the photos to the school newspaper—or even my uncle. He likes gliders. And we can pick up hints for our science project, right?"

"Right," Alex said. Looking around the field she said, "Chris told me he'd meet us at the main entrance to the gliderport terminal." From the parking lot, she could see three small gray hangars on the left side of the field, behind a long fence. Not far from the first hangar was an old yellow and brown building, with a small covered porch overlooking the grassy gliderport field. Alex walked a few steps to the right to see the sign on the roof: WINDSOCK FIELD TERMINAL.

"That's it," she called to the others, pointing toward the yellow building.

Chris stepped out of the terminal and stood on the porch, watching a plane pull a glider across the runway and into the sky. As Alex walked up the stairs to the terminal building, he turned and smiled. "Hey, Alex—you made it! You sure picked the right day to glide. And you have quite a group here."

"Yeah, they all wanted to come. This is my mother, Mrs. Mack. My dad, Mr. Mack. My sister, Annie. And you know everyone else."

Chris nodded to the group, then pointed to a white glider landing on the runway. "You're all in for a treat. That's Sam Hollenbeck in there. He's one of the best glider pilots and mechanics we have around here. He'll be taking you all up today. Come on, I'll show you guys what a glider looks like."

"Bathroom," Louis said suddenly. "Where's the bathroom, Chris?"

Chris pointed to the terminal door. "In there. To the left. Do you want us to wait?"

"Naw. I'll find you," said Louis, slipping quickly through the door.

Alex looked at Ray. "Do you get the idea he doesn't really want to do this?" she whispered to her friend. Ray shrugged and followed the others.

Chris led them to a glider sitting along the side of the runway and lifted the plane's plastic bubble canopy. Alex and the others listened as he quickly explained the parts of the glider: the pilot seat, the instruments to let the pilot know how high and fast the plane was flying, and the pedals and handles used to steer the plane. Alex was surprised—the glider seemed so bare. "Is that all there is to a glider?" she asked.

"Yeah," added Robyn. "I mean, isn't there a backup engine or something?"

Chris chuckled. "Believe me, you don't need one," he replied. "Who needs an engine when you have the air to hold you up? Now, who wants to go first?" Chris said, looking at Alex.

Suddenly, Alex grimaced and felt her stomach lurch. She'd been looking forward to this moment for days. But now that it was finally here . . . As she looked over at Robyn for some sign of support, her friend snapped the shutter of the camera. "Good shot, Alex. You've got the frightened look down, all right."

Alex bit on her nail. It wasn't that she didn't want to go up in the glider, but she was a little apprehensive—maybe a lot apprehensive. Before she could say anything to Chris, Mrs. Mack raised her hand and exclaimed, "I'll go!"

Alex looked over at her mother, surprised that she was willing to be the first one up. As Robyn continued to snap pictures with her camera, Chris escorted Barbara Mack to the waiting glider on the field. Suddenly, Alex realized that her *mother* was the one going into the glider—a plane with no engine and no brakes—and she wanted to be with her.

"Hey, Chris," Alex called out. "Can I go with my mom?"

Chris shook his head. "Nope. Only the pilot and one passenger. There's no room for anyone else."

Alex's hands began to sweat. She thought about the time she took an airplane to see her grandmother: the engine sounds, the other people on the plane, and even the stewardess who served her a root beer. That had been fun, and she'd been almost sad when the plane had landed. But here, there was only the pilot, her mother—and no engine.

Mrs. Mack didn't seem to have any doubts about getting into the glider. As Chris introduced her to the pilot and helped her aboard, she smiled and waved her notebook and pen. "Research for my paper!" she yelled back to the group. Everyone smiled and waved—except Alex.

Alex stood with the others on the side of the runway and watched as the tow plane pulled the glider. She could see her mother's head looking all around, and the pilot talking to her. A moment later, they were airborne. Alex watched as the glider became smaller and smaller.

"Does anyone want a drink?" Chris asked as he walked back to the group. Mr. Mack and Annie shook their heads and continued talking about gliders.

"Sure," said Ray, nudging Alex with his elbow. "You?"

Alex shook her head and continued to look up at the glider. She was afraid to let it out of her sight—as if staring at it would make it stay up.

"Well, I'm going to get one," Ray said. "I'm hot—and I bet I'll find Louis at the food counter. You coming, Robyn?"

"No, I'm shooting pictures, remember?"

As Ray and Chris turned toward the terminal, Chris hesitated and turned to Alex. "Alex, she'll be fine."

"I know," she heard her voice say.

* * *

Alex let out a sigh of relief when Mrs. Mack's glider sailed to a gentle landing twenty minutes later. "Mom?" asked Alex, practically running into her mother's arms as Mrs. Mack reached the group. "How was it?"

Mrs. Mack hugged Alex and giggled. "You wouldn't believe it." She sighed. "It's like riding on a cloud. And it's so peaceful. You can't hear anything but the wind blowing past the plane. And you can see everywhere around you."

Mrs. Mack kept her arm around Alex's shoulder. Everyone asked questions all at once, while Robyn snapped the camera at Mrs. Mack. "Hey, hon," said Mr. Mack. "You'd better write all of this down for your paper—you'll forget it."

"I don't think I'll forget it anytime soon," Mrs. Mack said, somewhat breathlessly. "It was fantastic."

As Chris and Ray joined the group again, Mr. Mack was next to volunteer. The afternoon seemed to drag by for Alex as she watched the others volunteer after Mr. Mack: Ray was next, then Annie.

"Hey, where's Louis?" asked Ray, grinning and standing next to Alex after his ride. "He's going to love this."

"He said he was hungry," Robyn answered, putting more film in her camera. "I saw him walk back into the terminal. He's probably looking for food like a crazed squirrel."

"The guy has a bottomless stomach," Ray said.

Alex's own stomach wasn't doing too well, either. Sure, she had watched her mom, dad, and Ray go on a glider ride—and they all seemed to have a great time. But Alex was a little afraid. *No, not really afraid,* she told herself, *just apprehensive. Well, okay, so I'm afraid,* she admitted silently. What if she did something wrong? What if the winds picked up? Maybe she should ask for a backup engine—just for her glider?

Alex shook her head—hard. *This is ridiculous,* she told herself. Annie was up there enjoying herself, and if her sister could do it, *she* could do it.

Alex paced in a circle while Annie's glider landed on the open runway. As the bubble canopy opened, she saw her sister wave—then laugh. That couldn't be her sister. Not her straight-faced sister who looked at everything with a scientific eye. She must be mistaken. Maybe aliens took over her sister's body while she was in the glider. "Hey, Robyn," she said, nudging her friend and pointing to Annie. "Be sure to get a picture of that—and I want an eight-by-ten glossy for my wall."

"Alex!" her sister shouted, ignoring Robyn's clicking camera as she ran up to her sister. "You *have* to do it. It's . . . it's unbelievable!"

Alex grimaced. "I know. But I just want to think about—"

"Your turn, Alex," Chris called.

Alex turned to Chris, took a deep breath, and walked across the grass toward the glider. Everything seemed to move in slow motion. She stopped and looked back at her parents. They smiled, and her mother blew her a kiss. Ray and Annie waved. And Robyn kept clicking her camera.

All she needed to do was turn around again and go to the glider. But it felt as if her feet were rooted to the spot. *Maybe I could use my powers to help us if we get into trouble,* she thought, then shook her head. As Annie often said, there were times when she couldn't rely on her powers.

"Come on, Alex. Mr. Hollenbeck is ready again." Chris gently took her arm and led her to the glider. "If it makes you feel any better," he added, "the Wright brothers' first flight only took twelve seconds—and the plane wasn't built half as well as the one you're going on."

Alex gulped. As they walked across the big grassy field, she could see mud splashed along the side of the shiny white glider. The small sailplane seemed to be tilted to one side, leaning on one of its large, long wings. Several yards in front of the glider was a small airplane, complete with motor. The sailplane was attached to the airplane with a long, bright yellow rope. "What did you call that?" asked Alex, pointing to the lead airplane.

"That's your tow plane. I'm afraid we can't toss this thing into the air like a paper airplane," Chris answered. Alex tried to smile. "And that Cessna is one of our best tow planes."

As they approached the glider, Alex saw Mr. Hollenbeck waiting for her. He was a big man, bald as well as beardless. He was wearing a bright red T-shirt, emblazoned with the words, "For a Wide Smile, Try a Glide Ride, Windsock Field." And he was taking the advice of his T-shirt: He had a big, wide smile.

"I'm Sam. You ready?" asked Mr. Hollenbeck, holding open the glider's bubble canopy.

Alex gulped again. "I'm Alex Mack." She turned to Chris. "Are you coming, too?"

"No, I'm just here to make sure you two are snug in the glider, and I'll be the wing-runner," he said, helping Alex into the cockpit. She settled in and noticed in front of her were the same instruments that the pilot used to operate the glider.

Chris helped her to strap in, and Mr. Hollenbeck climbed in behind her, instructing, "Don't touch that red knob until I tell you to—it's how we release the glider from the tow plane."

After Chris shut the bubble, she heard Mr. Hollenbeck fussing in the back. "What are you doing?" she asked, trying to turn in her seat. She didn't like it that she couldn't see him.

"Just take it easy, Alex. I'm adjusting myself back here and getting ready to roll," he answered. All of a sudden, she wished she were with someone who would talk more—she'd even take Annie at this point. All she wanted to do was ask questions, and she felt as if Mr. Hollenbeck were too busy to answer.

"If you have any questions, young lady, just ask away," Mr. Hollenbeck said, almost as if he read her mind.

"Thanks," was all she could think of to say. She tried to focus on something—anything to stop her heart from thumping: the instrument panel in front of her, the red knob at her side, even the seat belt. Then she looked down at her hands.

Oh, no, she thought. *Not now!* Alex's hands were beginning to glow.

CHAPTER 3

Alex was grateful that her seat in the glider was facing away from Mr. Hollenbeck. She looked at her hands again, and they were still glowing dimly, the way they did when she got nervous. She tucked them under her arms, trying to hide them as much as possible.

"Are you cold, Alex?"

Alex shook her head. "No," she said quickly, trying to stare straight ahead so Mr. Hollenbeck couldn't see her face, which was glowing as brightly as her hands.

The next few minutes seemed like a dream. The tow plane rolled forward and the yellow rope went taut. As the plane slowly dragged the glider, Chris ran alongside, holding up the right wing so it wouldn't scrape along the ground. When the wings leveled off, Chris let go, and the glider lifted just a few feet off the ground. As the tow plane reached the end of the runway, it lifted off. The glider gracefully tagged along behind and Alex felt a little pull in her stomach.

"We're flying, Alex!" Mr. Hollenbeck shouted as the glider sailed off the ground.

The sailplane rose above the treetops. Suddenly, the valley seemed to spread out before Alex, right beyond the nose of the glider. The sensation was different than when she was on the airplane to see her grandmother. Alex was surprised that she could see everything around her, not just out the window on one side of the plane. She could see open sky on either side of her and in front. When she looked up, the clouds seemed close enough to touch. And when she looked down, everything was so small: the cars, roads, cows, trains, barns, farmhouses, even people. It reminded her of a dollhouse and a train set she once had when she was younger.

But the biggest difference between the flight

and the one on the airplane—besides the fact that there was no flight attendant and no root beer—was the lack of noise. There was no loud motor and no people talking around her. The only thing Alex could hear was the wind whistling by the wings and bubble canopy. It was very peaceful, just as her mother had said. *Now I know how birds must feel,* she thought.

Alex knew she was gawking out the window, but she didn't care. Suddenly, she realized that Mr. Hollenbeck was talking to her. "I'm sorry, Mr. Hollenbeck. What did you say?"

Mr. Hollenbeck laughed. "You have first-time rider's ear-block," he said. "Everyone gets it when they first fly. Isn't it beautiful?"

"It's fantastic! Unbelievable!" Alex suddenly realized she was using the same terms that her parents, sister, and Ray had used. And she also knew the words really weren't strong enough to describe the experience.

"Now, when I give the word, pull that red knob on your left. It will release us from the towline and the plane," Mr. Hollenbeck explained.

Alex hesitated. She looked down at her hands, afraid that they would still be glowing. But instead, they were back to normal—and she realized she was no longer nervous.

"Okay, pull the red knob—now!" Mr. Hollenbeck yelled.

When Alex pulled the button, it sounded like a firecracker exploding. As the towline released, the sailplane veered to the right, while the tow plane, with the line trailing behind, flew to the left. The plane smoothed out, and all Alex could hear was the wind whistling around her.

Suddenly Alex felt a jolt through her seat cushion. "Hold on, Alex. We found a thermal!"

"Thermal?" she asked, as she heard Mr. Hollenbeck push some levers behind her to steer the plane. The left wing dipped down, and the plane turned to her left.

"How do you feel?" said Mr. Hollenbeck as they moved in a tight circle.

"Great," she said. Leaning sideways into the turn made her stomach feel a little funny, but she was enjoying the view too much to really notice.

"The bump you felt was a rising air current, or a thermal," Mr. Hollenbeck explained. "In order to gain altitude, we have to turn toward it and stay with it. It's taking us up like an elevator—and if you look at that altimeter in front of you, you'll see how high we are now."

Alex remembered what Chris had told her about the various instruments on the glider. She looked at the airspeed indicator to see how fast they were traveling; then the variometer to see if they were going up or down. But the altimeter surprised her: It read 2,567 feet—they were almost a half-mile high! "Wow," she said. "Make that double wow."

The rest of the ride seemed to rush by too fast. Mr. Hollenbeck pointed out several sites that Alex recognized: the Paradise Valley Mall, the junior and senior high schools, and the main route through town. Alex tried to see her house, but it was hard to pick out her street and house from so far away. Eventually, Mr. Hollenbeck headed back for Windsock Field.

"And of course," he said, as they approached the field, "in front of us is Paradise Valley Chemical."

High above the plant, Alex didn't feel the usual lurch in her stomach. In the sailplane, it felt as if she were *above* worrying about the GC-161 or Danielle Atron. It was strange to find herself actually feeling safer up in the air than on the ground. The freedom was exhilarating. "Do we have to go back?" she asked.

Mr. Hollenbeck chuckled. "Pretty neat, huh?"

Alex smiled and nodded. Secretly she thought, *Wouldn't it be something if my powers actually allowed me to fly?*

The glider landed on the grassy runway. Chris ran up and raised the bubble when the plane rolled to a stop. "Chris, you were right," she said, stepping from the glider. "It was great! I didn't want to come down! Can we go up again?"

Chris laughed and pointed to the terminal. "Maybe another time. It's pretty late and we still have to get Louis up there."

Alex suddenly felt like a complete dork. She knew she sounded like a little kid at an amusement park. But she suddenly didn't care. Gliding *did* feel as if she were riding on a cloud. And it was exciting.

Everyone began walking back to the terminal porch. As Alex and Chris caught up, he looked around and asked, "Mrs. Mack, have you seen Louis?"

"Why, no." She turned to Mr. Mack. "Did you see him, George?"

"He was just here," he said, looking around.

"He said he was going back to the car to get his jacket. He was getting cold now that the sun was going down."

"Should I go look for him?" asked Alex.

"He'll be back, Alex," said Mrs. Mack, looking over at the terminal's café. "Right now, I think we should all get something to eat. It's close to dinner."

About fifteen minutes later, Louis appeared in the café. "Hi, guys. Did I miss anything?"

"Yeah. The last ride," said Ray, polishing off a hot dog.

"Sorry, Louis. I think your luck ran out," Chris said between bites of his hamburger. "It's a bit too late for another ride. We try not to send out gliders so close to dusk. Not enough good thermals left."

"Hey, that's okay. I understand," he said, reaching for a bag of potato chips. "I decided to go last because I wanted all of you to enjoy the fun of soaring. I really, really wanted to go, believe me. But I wanted all of you to enjoy yourselves first. I'll go next time."

Alex and Ray exchanged glances. She just *knew* Louis was trying to get out of flying all day. And she knew Ray knew, too.

"Age before beauty, and all that," Louis added.

"You're a real beauty, all right," Ray retorted.

After the last potato chip was eaten, everyone headed for the Macks' car. Alex was still talking with her mother about the glider flight, her mother scribbling in her notebook as they walked. As Alex got closer to the car, she heard someone calling her.

"Alex—wait up." It was Chris.

Alex and Mrs. Mack stopped and turned to Chris. "Hey, Chris. I can't thank you enough for asking us up here," Alex said.

"Yeah, no problem. Uh, Alex, I was wondering," Chris said, looking at Mrs. Mack, then at Alex. "Would . . . would you like to go to the mall with me tomorrow? You know, just to walk around?"

"Mom?"

Mrs. Mack smiled, waved her hand, and said, "Sure. No problem."

As her mother turned and walked back to the car, Alex shook her head. "Gee," she muttered, "maybe now's the time to ask for a raise in my allowance."

"Naw. Start by asking for a new car. Then work your way down," Chris said.

They both laughed. Alex realized she was growing more comfortable around Chris. He had a great sense of humor, and she was starting to like being with him.

"I'll meet you at the mall about eleven," he said. "By the sunglasses booth."

Alex nodded and waved her hand. "Okay. See ya."

CHAPTER 4

Mr. Mack dropped Alex off at the Paradise Valley Mall the next day just in time to meet Chris. The day was hot and humid, and she had had a hard time deciding what to wear. She finally settled on a sleeveless white blouse, tan shorts, and brown sandals—and her hair in a braid to keep it off her neck. As she walked to the sunglasses stand, Alex felt as if she had dragged the hot air in with her.

"Is it hot in here or what?" Chris asked as she walked up to him. "Feels like they turned off the air-conditioning."

"Or it's out of whack," said Alex, waving her

hand in front of her face like a fan. For a moment, she thought it would be great to send a zapper into the air-conditioning system. *Nice try, Alex,* she thought, *expose your powers just because you're hot.* Instead, she changed the subject. "I'd like to be up in a glider right now—with the windows open."

Chris laughed. "I don't think you'd want to do that, Alex. Talk about wind burn," he said, starting to walk down the mall. "You know, if people knew how much fun soaring really was, there would be more people wanting to fly. I just wish . . ." Chris hesitated.

Alex turned to look at Chris as they walked. "Wish what?" she prompted.

"Well, there's something I didn't tell you," Chris said, stopping and looking at a display in front of a bookstore window. "It's about my dad. He owns Windsock Field."

Alex's eyes went wide. "He *owns* it?"

Chris took a deep breath, then looked at Alex. "Yeah. He started a soaring school when we moved here, and ever since, he's been trying desperately to keep it going and get it accredited. I would have introduced you to him yesterday, but as usual, he was in the office all day talking to inspectors and officials over the phone. I think the school's in trouble. But you know parents; they don't tell us kids certain things. They think we don't know anything," he said, frustration in his voice.

"Yeah. My parents can be the same way," Alex said, thinking about how her parents seemed to end certain conversations very abruptly when she walked in the room.

"Aren't they all . . ." Chris hesitated. He looked over Alex's shoulder and smiled. "Robyn . . . Nicole . . . where did you come from?"

Alex turned. Standing behind her were her two good friends. She wanted to know more about Chris's father and the field, but realized it was the wrong time to continue the subject.

"Hi, Alex . . . Chris. It's boil city around here," said Nicole, using a magazine to fan herself.

"Yeah, I think the air-conditioning is broken," said Chris, running his hand through his short hair. "It happens here once in a while, especially when it's real hot outside."

"Hey, outside reminds me," said Robyn. She pulled out three rolls of film and held them up. "I'm here to drop off the film I took yesterday. I tried to snap shots of everyone as they went up in the glider and then when they came off the glider."

"Who went up?" asked Nicole.

"My mom, dad, and sister, Ray, and me," Alex responded.

"Yeah, it looked like fun," said Robyn. "A little scary, though, if you ask me. I'm sure the pilot was qualified, but just in case, maybe I'll take parachute lessons before I ever go up."

Nicole looked at Robyn. "You didn't go up?"

"No," Alex answered for her friend. "She was our official photographer. And I hope you got Annie with that smile on her face. Maybe we could sell it to the newspapers as a world-shaking event. I just felt real sorry for poor Louis—he missed the last ride."

"He couldn't stop eating," Chris added.

"Sounds like Louis," said Nicole. She impatiently pushed a dark lock of hair from her forehead. "I'd love to hear about your adventures, guys, but I have to get my hair cut. It's dry. It's hot. And these bangs are driving me crazy."

"Too bad. And we were just about to go for some lunch at Pizza Platter." Alex turned to her other friend. "Want to join us, Robyn?"

"Nope. Thanks anyway. I have to drop off the film, then meet my dad at the sporting store.

He's taking me to my cousin's baseball game this afternoon. The Rockets versus the Hawks. Some kind of exhibition or something. I just hope I have enough sunscreen," she said, absently looking through her overstuffed purse.

Alex smiled, knowing Robyn always had plenty of sunscreen with her, wherever she went. "Robyn, something in there is going to attack you one day," said Alex, pretending to peer inside the purse.

"Ha! You just wait. Someday you'll need something from this thing and you'll thank me," Robyn said, snapping the purse shut and putting the strap back on her shoulder.

Alex was about to reply when she saw a man in a brown leather jacket accidentally bump into a young child in front of a nearby clothing store. It wasn't the jostling that caught her eye, but the man's cap. The hat was shaped like a baseball cap. It was dark blue with gold "scrambled eggs" trim, and read USS *Ohio*. She had heard about the navy submarine before, from a special program on television. *Now that hat would make a nice addition to my collection,* she thought, then shook her head. She already had too many hats in her collection. Annie was threatening to donate them to a worthy cause, such as the Bald and Beautiful Club of Seattle.

Alex turned back to her friends, and as they all said their good-byes, she began to wonder about what Chris had said earlier. But she didn't know him well enough to bring up the subject. She wanted him to tell her on his own.

"You're really lucky to have such close friends," said Chris as they walked to the Pizza Platter. "I wish I had more friends."

"You do—I noticed them at the soaring field."

"Yeah. But they're my soaring friends. And my dad's friends. I'd just like some of my own."

"Ray and Louis are your friends. And so am I," she added helpfully.

"Thanks," he said, turning to her and smiling. "Hey, how about that pizza? Do you want anything on it?"

As the man behind the counter took their order, Alex looked around for a table. Just as she found one near the door, the man with the dark blue cap slipped into a seat nearby. He had a glass of soda and a small slice of pizza in front of him, but he didn't take off his cap or jacket as he ate. Alex thought it was strange. Certainly it was hot in the mall—why would anyone be wearing a leather jacket in such hot weather?

Alex froze as another thought crossed her mind: Was it her imagination, or was this man following her? And if he was following her, was he from Paradise Valley Chemical, looking for the kid who was doused with GC-161? Was he waiting for her to slip up and use her powers?

"Well, I think my dad's soaring school is in trouble," Chris said as they sat down. He bit into a slice of pizza, swallowed, then took a sip of soda. "He hasn't been too happy lately, and he yells a lot over the phone. That's not like him at all."

Alex nodded, chewing her pizza. Every now and then, she slipped a glance toward the man in the cap, but she still couldn't see his face.

"I know it's the developers who keep calling—Ace Developers—you've seen their place. They're just down the street from school," Chris continued. "They really bugged him at the end of last semester to sell the place. And I know he won't let that happen. I won't let that happen."

"But what can you do?"

"I don't know. Maybe get a part-time job. You know, make some extra money for the soaring school. Maybe I can mow lawns," Chris said, putting the half-eaten pizza on his plate. "If I could only convince the inspectors that the school was one of the best—that we were really good at what we do. Then we'd have accreditation. If that happened, we'd get more business and wouldn't have to worry about developers."

Alex nodded. She watched as the man in the cap picked up his tray. He walked over to the garbage can, dumped his trash, then walked out of the Pizza Platter. She squinted, but she still couldn't see his face.

"Ummm . . . I have to go to the bathroom, Chris. I'll be right back," Alex said. As she pretended to turn into the ladies' room, she stopped. Looking back, she could see across the hallway and into the mall office.

One of the officials of the mall was talking to the man in the navy cap. And he, in turn, was pointing in the direction of Chris and Alex's table. Both men turned—and looked straight at Alex.

She ran back to the table and skidded to a stop. "Chris. Want to go now?" she asked, talking rapidly and pulling on his shirtsleeve. "This way. We'll go out the back door. I'm really hot, and it's cooler outside. I'm positive. Okay? Let's go!"

Confused, Chris was just able to push his trash

in the garbage before Alex dragged him into the hot sunshine. "You really believe in eating and running, don't you," he said.

Alex looked back and noticed no one was following. She sighed deeply. "Nope. Just running. Let's go wait for my dad."

CHAPTER 5

Alex was puzzled.

Why was the man in the navy cap pointing at her yesterday? Was he a security guard at the mall? Maybe he thought she stole something. Or maybe he *was* a spy from the chemical plant, trying to find out more about her. Maybe he even had a hidden GC-161 detector, and he suspected that she was the kid who—

"Earth to Alex. Are you listening?" asked Robyn.

Alex jumped in her seat. "Yeah, yeah, I'm listening. And melting." She couldn't say what was *really* on her mind. It would only bring up a difficult subject—her and her powers, which she couldn't discuss with even Robyn and Nicole.

It was Monday morning, and she was in one of her favorite classes: study hall, which was held in the cafeteria. Robyn, Nicole, and Chris sat across from her, and Louis and Ray on either side of Alex. But today, study hall wasn't her favorite class because the big cafeteria was one of the hottest rooms in the school, especially with the ovens cooking food for lunch. Everyone was wearing shorts and T-shirts, but it still didn't seem to help.

"Does it feel like we're in the Sahara Desert?" said Ray to no one in particular, wiping his forehead on his T-shirt sleeve.

"I think they should turn the ovens off and just serve ice cream for lunch," Louis said.

All period long, Alex and Robyn had been trying to work out the best paper airplane design based on the photos Robyn took at the soaring field. Alex had put together the main part of the flyer, and Robyn was drawing patterns on the plane, using examples from the gliders at Windsock Field.

At the beginning of study hall, Alex had persuaded Chris to tell the others about the trouble at his dad's soaring school. He hesitated at first, but Alex convinced him that maybe someone would have a good suggestion to help the school.

"So why do the developers want the land at the soaring school?" Robyn asked, reaching over for a red marker.

"Maybe Paradise Chemical wants it," Nicole suggested. Alex squirmed in her seat at the mention of the chemical plant, then turned back to her paper airplane. "The plant is right nearby," Nicole continued. "And it sounds like something they'd do. Expansion is their middle name."

"Maybe," said Chris. "But I don't think the plant is close enough to want to take over the field. I was thinking somebody else wants to put something on it. Hey, Louis, can I borrow your blue pen?"

"Yeah, here," said Louis, handing his ballpoint pen to Chris. "You mean like houses—or maybe even some new fast-food places?" asked Louis, tilting his head.

Chris opened up his notebook and started writing. "I wish I knew."

"And I wish there was some way we could help, Chris." Alex leaned her elbows on the cafeteria table and blew her hair out of her face.

"Yeah. But how?" Chris asked. "What we need is more people to notice the school."

Alex and the others were silent for a moment. "So what's the best way to get people to notice something?" she finally asked, looking around at each one of her friends.

Ray sat up in his chair. "Give them free chocolate? And in this case, in the shape of a glider?"

As the others started to laugh, Alex stared at her friend. "Ray, that's not a bad idea."

"It's not?" asked Louis, who was laughing the loudest.

A student in the back of the room glared at Louis and said, "Shhh . . . I'm trying to read."

"I think Ray's idea isn't half bad, if we change it a little," Alex continued, lowering her voice. She leaned forward in her chair. "Listen. Why can't we have a picnic, or party . . . or something we can call a 'field day' at the gliderport? We can invite the entire town and sell stuff like brownies and pizza. It won't cost much if we make it like a bake sale. We can get some other kids to help, and all of us can make stuff to eat—"

"And we could sell balloons—" added Robyn.

"And the soaring pilots can offer rides. We

can charge half price, and still earn some extra money," Chris said eagerly.

"Yeah, and it would let everyone know that the school exists," said Nicole.

"Great idea, Alex," said Chris. He slowly sat back in his seat, his smile suddenly fading. "There's one gigantic problem. I have to convince my dad."

Alex smiled. "And I know how." As the change of class bell rang, she added, "Everyone meet me at the front entrance after school."

"Umm . . . I have something to do after school," said Louis as he packed his math book in his backpack. "I'll catch you all later."

Alex frowned at Ray as Louis ran out the cafeteria door. "Why is he always doing a disappearing act lately?" she asked Ray. Ray just shrugged.

George Mack leaned down and finished drying off his just-washed car. On the other side of the car, Annie Mack was cleaning the passenger side window. They looked up as Alex, Robyn, Nicole, Chris, and Ray approached.

"Party? Or are you all volunteering to vacuum the car and scrub the tires?" asked Annie, squirting the glass cleaner on the window.

"Dream on, Annie," Alex said.

"We're the ones who need to be hosed down, anyway," Ray said, wiping the sweat off his brow.

"Well, all I can say is that you've got perfect timing," said Mr. Mack, wringing out a bright red rag. "Why is it that kids always show up *after* I've finished washing the car?"

Alex turned to her father and said, "Dad. What are you doing home so early?"

"I took a half day to finish off some of those chores that just won't go away," Mr. Mack said.

"Well, I'm glad you're home early," Alex said. " 'Cause we have an idea, but we don't know quite how to get it going. Can we ask your opinion on something?"

"I'm all ears," said Mr. Mack.

"We're trying to help Chris's dad keep his soaring school open, but they need to attract more people. At least we think he does. So we thought maybe we'd arrange a field day—"

"Sort of a plane party," Robyn interjected.

"Yeah," Alex continued. "But we don't know how to approach Mr. Gordon so he'll say yes."

"How about just asking him outright?" Mr. Mack suggested. "And I don't think he'd mind at all. I remember your dad when he used to work at Paradise Valley Chemical, Chris."

"He worked *there?*" Alex asked, startled. She looked at Chris.

Chris nodded as Mr. Mack continued. "Bud Gordon used to work as an engineer at the plant a few years ago, but he always wanted to start a soaring school, not bow to the chemical plant's whims. I know your family moved to Oklahoma for a while." Chris nodded in reply. "I guess he flew all kinds of planes while he was there," Mr. Mack continued, "and now he's back. I thought I heard he bought the old field at Windsock. There used to be a great deal of soaring up there years ago."

"And now he's turned it into a soaring school," Chris added. "But he needs accreditation—and that means people have to show up, Mr. Mack. "He has to log hours, and demonstrate a student base."

"Well, I think you kids have a fine idea," Mr. Mack said, turning to Alex. "Do you want me to drive you up there so you can talk with Mr. Gordon?"

Alex nodded without hesitation. "Can we all go?"

"Sure—pile into the car," said Mr. Mack.

"Not me," said Annie. "I'm going to do some homework."

Mr. Mack walked to the house, relayed his plans to Mrs. Mack, then hopped in the car. Alex jumped in the passenger seat, then turned to the others as they squeezed into the backseat. "Just don't get fingerprints on the windows. Annie just cleaned them."

As they traveled to the field, everyone seemed to be talking at once about soaring, a field day, and how to approach Mr. Gordon.

Sam Hollenbeck was just getting into his car in the soaring field's parking lot when the Mack car drove up. As they all gathered around, Chris quickly explained the plan to Mr. Hollenbeck. The pilot nodded his approval. "Sounds good to me," he said, leading them inside the main terminal office. Sitting behind a desk was a handsome man dressed in a white shirt and tie, his dark brown hair and mustache matching his deep brown eyes. Mr. Hollenbeck nodded to the man, then pointed to the group. "Bud, these young people would like a word with you."

Mr. Gordon slowly stood up, looking at Chris with a puzzled expression. "Chris, is everything all right?"

"Yeah, Dad," he said. "We'd just like to talk to you about something."

"Okay." As he put his pen down on the desk, Alex could see him let out a relieved sigh. "Well, if it isn't George Mack," he said, his face lighting up as he suddenly noticed Alex's father in the back. "How are you, George?"

Both men shook hands. "Great, Bud. I see you've really done well for yourself," said Mr. Mack, smiling as he looked around the office.

"Beats working for the chemical plant," he said, putting his hands on his hips. "Now what's this all about, Chris?"

"Umm, well—"

"I'll tell him, Chris," Alex interrupted. After all, it was her idea. Chris smiled at Alex, then nodded. "We have a proposal to make to you, Mr. Gordon," she said. "We know you've been trying to get more people out here, to help your school and all. We thought we might help by having a field day here."

Mr. Gordon frowned and looked at Chris. "Was this your idea?"

"No, we all came up with the idea, Mr. Gordon. Chris is a good friend and we just want to help," said Alex, pulling out a piece of paper from her back pocket. "See? We've worked out kind of a schedule and what we need to do. I know we can be ready by this Saturday. With everybody pitching in, it shouldn't be too much work. And we could call it a 'Field Awareness Day,' " she added, handing the paper to Mr. Gordon.

"Hey, that's it! We can call it FAD," Ray commented, folding his arms in front of his chest. "I like it. 'Tired of the usual fads? Come to our FAD!' "

Alex, Robyn, and Nicole all rolled their eyes at each other. But Alex had to smile. Ray's comment seemed to cut the tension in the room.

Mr. Gordon looked at the paper, then ran his hand through his short hair. "It's really a nice idea, kids, but I can't see where we'd possibly make any money—and I can't afford to spend any. Not only that, the air-conditioning unit in the main hangar just conked out for some reason. Plus, I just cut back everyone's salary and benefits about a month ago so I could keep us open long enough to get accreditation. I don't know if my pilots will be willing to put in the overtime without getting paid."

"But, Dad, a field day would bring in more people," Chris pleaded. "Isn't that what we really need right now to keep the school going?"

Mr. Gordon shook his head again. "But can you all handle a field day on such short notice?"

"I know these kids, Bud. They really want to help," added Mr. Mack, leaning against a filing cabinet. "And they're all good workers."

"Well, they all have my vote, Bud," Mr. Hollenbeck said. "It would be fun—plus, think of all the publicity. And I'm sure the other pilots would agree."

"Oh, I don't know," said Mr. Gordon. He turned to a huge calendar behind his desk and rubbed his chin. "Nope. Saturday won't work. That's when the inspectors arrive. We just can't handle everything at once." He turned to Chris and the others. "I'm sorry, kids. Maybe some other time."

Chewing on her lip, Alex stared at the floor. She had to convince Mr. Gordon that the only way to bring people to the school was to invite them. And the only way to prove to the inspectors that the school would be a success was to . . .

"That's perfect!" said Alex. Everyone turned to her, looking at her as if she had grown three heads. "Don't you see? We can show the inspectors the best that the field has to offer. If we have the field day at the same time they're here, you can show them that everyone in Paradise

Valley is interested in soaring at Windsock Field!"

Mr. Gordon nodded slowly. "I see what you're saying. If the inspectors saw all the people interested in the field and the school, they might be more agreeable to giving me the accreditation." Mr. Gordon seemed to stand up straighter. "It just might work," he said, smiling broadly. Putting his hand out to Alex, he said, "Young lady, you have yourself a deal."

Alex shook Mr. Gordon's hand and pulled out another list from her pocket. She handed it to Mr. Gordon. "First, we'll do all of the baking and sign-making. Second, we'll need handouts to advertise the event."

"We can use the copier to make handouts," said Mr. Hollenbeck, pointing to the machine in the corner of the office.

"Robyn and I can hand out the copies at school and in grocery stores," added Nicole. Robyn nodded.

"My mom said she'd be glad to help us, too, and she's going to lend us the tent and cash box she used for her garage sale," Alex said. "And finally, Mr. Gordon, can you arrange for your people to give soaring rides?"

"No problem with that. We'd have to do it when the inspectors were here anyway."

Mr. Gordon and Chris walked the group out to the Macks' car. Alex looked back at the terminal and asked, "Ray, isn't that Louis over there—on the porch?"

Ray turned and looked toward the building. "Yeah. It sure looks like him. What's he doing out here?"

"Maybe he came to join us," she said, waving her hand. "Hey, Louis!"

Louis turned for a second in their direction, then ran back into the terminal. Ray looked at Alex and shrugged. "Maybe it wasn't him."

"Come on, kids," announced Mr. Mack. "Time to go."

Alex walked around the Macks' car, then turned toward the hangar on the far side of the field. It was sunset, but she thought she saw something, possibly a man's silhouette. As everyone piled into the car, she squinted in the direction of the movement. Was it Louis again?

There, slipping around the back of a hangar, was a figure moving quickly through the shadows. As a dim beam of sunlight struck the person, Alex could see clearly for a moment. But before she could say anything, the movement was gone.

She shivered. The figure was wearing a brown leather jacket—and a dark cap decorated with a yellow braid! It was the same person she thought was spying on her in the mall!

CHAPTER 6

Alex was deep in thought as she walked to class. For the past two days, she had been thinking, not only about the field day, but about the strange man in the dark blue hat. *If he's just eavesdropping, hoping to catch me saying something about GC-161,* she thought, *then he's a pretty poor substitute for Dave, Vince, or Lars.* At least the employees of Paradise Valley Chemical tried harder—especially to stay out of sight. This man was right out in the open.

She had already told Ray and Annie about the mysterious man, and they had the same reaction: Be careful.

Alex tried to push aside the image of the strange man and his navy cap. There were too many other things to concentrate on at the moment—like school. It was Wednesday, and time for her science lab. As she settled into her seat, she watched Robyn pull the finished paper airplane out from an old shoe box. "I'm pretending the box is its hangar," she said, putting the plane in front of Alex.

Alex chuckled. She was glad that Robyn was around, not only to help with the science project, but later on, to help her plan the Field Awareness Day festivities. After all, Robyn had been in charge of the Valentine's Day dance a couple years ago at the school, so at least she knew how to organize. Alex also thought it was nice to have someone to sympathize with her when things got a little crazy.

Alex looked up as Mrs. Dellia asked the first student to throw his paper airplane. The plane flew over the head of his lab partner then landed upside down on the front desk. The next team's airplane took a nosedive, splashing into the science lab's aquarium. The paper airplane of the third team just fell out of the student's hand and crashed to the floor.

"All right, Alan. That's a very interesting

paper airplane, even if it didn't fly," Mrs. Dellia commented. "Remember, class. It's important that the plane flies, but it's even more important that the airplane has a design that is well thought out. I think everyone has done great so far. So, who's next?" She checked her clipboard and looked up. "Alexandra Mack and Robyn Russo?"

Alex and Robyn stood up and walked to the front of the class. They had agreed the night before to dress up for their presentation—Robyn wearing a white blouse with a black jumper, and Alex wearing her new plaid blouse and tan skirt. Alex cleared her throat. "Our airplane is called the 'Windsock High Flyer,' " she said, glancing quickly at Chris. "It's based on the principles we learned while flying in—"

"And taking pictures of—" Robyn added.

"—the sailplanes at Windsock Field," Alex concluded.

Robyn held up the paper airplane, then handed it to Alex. It was white with a red stripe down the side, similar to the one Alex had ridden at Windsock Field.

Just as Alex pulled her arm back to throw the plane, Robyn started talking. "One feature that I wanted to add was a lightning rod. But," she said, "Alex had a good point: Why would I want to *attract* lightning to a plane? So I added a radio antenna instead." She pointed to the thin paper rod sticking up from the middle of the glider. The class laughed as Alex raised her eyebrows at Robyn, impatient to begin. "I'm done," Robyn said. "You can toss it."

Alex pulled back her arm again and threw the plane. She held her breath as the flyer seemed to hover for a second. Then it floated gracefully past Ray and Louis, over the heads of three more students, banked gently to the left past Chris—and landed right at the feet of Mrs. Dellia.

Robyn grabbed Alex's arm. "It was the radio antenna—I just know it," she exclaimed, clapping her hands together.

Alex laughed and ran for the plane, realizing that the entire class was clapping. As Alex and Robyn went back to their seats, Ray and Louis gave them both high-fives. Alex caught Chris's eye and he gave her the thumbs-up sign.

"Nicely done, Alex and Robyn," said Mrs. Dellia. "Looks like watching the sailplanes at Windsock Field certainly helped."

"Ummm . . . Mrs. Dellia?" said Alex, raising her hand.

"Yes?"

"One more thing," she said, putting on her best selling voice. "There's going to be a Field Awareness Day—or FAD," she said, glancing at Ray, "at Windsock Field this Saturday from ten A.M. to three P.M. Everyone's invited. There'll be food, sailplane rides, and more food."

"Okay, now—"

"And did I say sailplane rides?" Alex said, turning to Robyn. Her friend nodded. "They're really awesome," Alex continued. "Really, I went up—"

"Uh, right, Alex. Thank you," Mrs. Dellia interrupted. "But I think we've all seen the signs up in the hallway."

"You mean those fancy, fluorescent posters painted with such skill and artistic vision?" Louis blurted out.

"Yes, Louis. The posters that seem to be plastered everywhere," said Mrs. Dellia. "There was even one on the ceiling of the Teacher's Lounge. Couldn't miss it."

"Yeah," he said, looking at his nails. "That was quite a feat. And not only that, I painted all the posters myself—with a little help from Ray."

"*Little* help?" Ray repeated incredulously. "*I* was the one who—"

"All right, Mr. Alvarado," Mrs. Dellia said.

"Why don't you and Louis show us your paper airplane."

Ray glared at Louis as they walked to the front of the class. Alex half-listened as Ray described the Wondersonic Space Shuttle. But she sat up as he threw his arm back and launched the plane. The Wondersonic flew up rapidly—then struck the ceiling, crushing the front of the plane. Alex winced as it fell to the ground with a thud.

"Ray? Louis?" said Mrs. Dellia.

"Yes, ma'am?" they said in unison, staring down at what was left of the plane.

"Maybe you should stick to painting signs."

Alex finished the last of her lunch, then pushed the tray away. She leaned over the table and listened intently to Chris.

"You heard about the air conditioner at the main hangar the other day. And yesterday the sprinkler system went crazy," he said, crumpling up a paper napkin and throwing it onto his tray. "Water was running over everything. Some of the glider canopies were open, but we did manage to shut them up before the seats and consoles got ruined."

She sat with Chris in the cafeteria, listening as he relayed all the things that had gone wrong at the field in the past month. Chris's father had noticed some important papers missing from the front seat of his car. Soon after that, the main hangar's automatic door opener went on the blink. And now the broken air-conditioning and sprinkler system. She felt bad for Chris and his father, but she didn't know what to do. It seemed as if everything were going wrong for Windsock Field. Alex sighed and rested her head in her left hand.

"I'm sorry. I guess I'm going on forever," Chris said, twisting a drinking straw.

Alex shrugged, saying, "That's okay."

"Congratulations on your science project. Your plane was the only one that really flew," Chris said.

"Yeah. And guess what?" she said, thinking a change in subject might help cheer Chris up. "Mrs. Dellia told me I can do my next science project on Amelia Earhart. I get to research her life as a pilot."

"Cool! She's my favorite pilot. Her plane disappeared over the South Pacific, and it's still a mystery as to what happened to her."

"Yeah. All the way back in 1937. She was pretty brave, if you ask me," Alex answered.

"What a bummer she didn't make it around the world."

"Speaking of bummers," Chris said, his eyes shifting around the room. "My dad finally told me what the developers want to do with the field—they want to build a mall!"

"You're kidding! How did you find out?"

"I asked. I told my dad that I knew the developers had been around, so he finally let me in on what's going on," Chris said.

"This may seem like a strange question, but did the developer ever wear a brown leather jacket and a dark blue cap that had USS *Ohio* on it?" Alex asked, hopeful that she would solve at least one bothersome problem.

"No, not that I remember. Why do you ask?"

"Oh, no reason. Just curious," Alex said, suddenly feeling discouraged. She thought just maybe one of the developers would be the man in the dark blue cap. But even if he was, what would he want with her?

CHAPTER 7

Study hall was Alex and Ray's last class of the day on Friday. Alex could barely stand the apprehension before the big day at the soaring field, and she had so much left to do that her head was spinning. Not only did she have a definite knot in her stomach, but time seemed to be at a standstill. Every now and then, she would look up at the clock, then look at Ray. He was slouching in his seat, also watching the clock.

After about twenty minutes of nail biting, toe tapping, and pencil chewing, he leaned over to Alex. "Do you think we can get rid of that clock?" he whispered. "It's making me nervous. And the hour and minute hands haven't moved for days."

Alex nodded in reply. She knew just how he felt. Time seemed to be going much slower than it should. "Maybe if we study," she whispered back. "After all, this is a study hall."

"I can't concentrate," he grumbled. "All I can think about is: Did I remember everything I was supposed to bring to the airfield tonight."

"Me, too. Oh, did you remember the spatula?"

Ray nodded.

"And four of your grandmother's aprons?" she said, her voice becoming a little louder. "I know we'll need them, especially when we hand out the pizza."

Ray nodded again. "And I remembered the ketchup," he said, ticking each item off with his fingers, "and the mustard, and the relish, and the beach towel."

"Ray," she asked, staring at her best friend. "A beach towel?"

"Yeah," he said, with a half-smile. "On my breaks, I may want to lie out and watch the girls walk by."

"What?"

"Shhhhhh . . ." said a girl sitting behind Ray. "I'm trying to study."

Alex scowled at Ray and opened her assigned book for English. So far, she had enjoyed reading *Gulliver's Travels.* It was Jonathan Swift's great adventure story about a traveler among giants and the tiny Lilliputians, talking horses, and flying islands—but she knew the book was really a comment on human society. She read the first paragraph then reread the first paragraph. After about ten more minutes, Alex realized that all she was doing was reading the same paragraph over and over—and she still didn't know what it said. *That's it,* she thought, *I give up. Maybe I won't be too tired to do my homework on Sunday—because I sure can't think about it now.*

When the bell for the end of class finally rang, Alex—with Ray in tow—practically flew home. Annie was on the telephone, answering questions about the field day, in between making chocolate chip and peanut butter cookies. Robyn and Louis were already there and not long after, Chris and Nicole arrived.

Alex turned to Annie when she got off the phone and asked with a touch of panic in her voice, "Where's Mom and Dad?"

"They went out to get some change for the cash box. And I think dinner," she answered as the telephone began to ring again. " 'Scuse me. Duty calls."

Alex watched the chaos around her. Her friends were either making decorations, moving boxes, looking for places to put pans, paper, or food, or dropping things. And it seemed as if everyone were talking at once. *This would be a great time to use my powers. Then again, with everyone around, this would be a very bad time to use my powers,* she thought, watching her friends work at a frantic pace.

As she worked, Alex tried to keep track of everyone around her, but it was very confusing. Ray was trying to wrap all the food, while making sure that Annie's cookies were tested to their utmost. Chris was trying to pack everything neatly and orderly in the many boxes around the room. Everything seemed to be working out just fine. That is, until Robyn insisted on making the cupcakes from scratch—which took much longer than the mix.

Then Louis wanted to chip in, too, insisting on frosting the cupcakes. Robyn started to protest when Louis grabbed a cupcake and started spreading the frosting. It melted instead of staying on top of the cupcake.

Robyn slapped his hand. "See? You don't even know that you don't frost until they're cold."

"Well, I guess I'll just have to eat this one, since I've ruined it. What a shame," he said with a grin, and then took a big bite.

Alex turned from Robyn and Louis to the voices raising in volume behind her. *Now what?* she thought.

"All I have to do is follow the box directions, Nicole," Ray was saying, holding a nine-by-thirteen-inch pan in his hands.

"No, I'll do the brownies," said Nicole, pulling the pan from Ray's hands.

"Oh, no, you don't," Ray answered, pulling the pan back.

"Chill, Ray! Nicole!" Alex finally said, stepping between her two friends.

"Yeah, kids, play nicely," said Annie. She was sitting in a chair pulled safely to the side of the room, contentedly watching—and enjoying, Alex noticed—the chaos around her.

The door burst open before Alex could comment. In came Mr. and Mrs. Mack, complete with the cash box and a huge bag. Alex looked into the bag and saw a healthy supply of chicken, salad, and rolls for dinner.

"Dinner's here!" Mrs. Mack called, waving a chicken bucket in front of Louis's nose. "Interest you in a piece of chicken, Louis?"

"Sure," came the reply. He set down his half-eaten cupcake and, without hesitation, grabbed a piece of chicken.

"Glad you're home, Mom," Alex said. "It was getting pretty hairy in here."

Everyone started reaching for pieces of chicken. "I figured it would be," Mrs. Mack answered. She took a chicken piece and licked her fingers. "All you have to do is remember to feed the animals once in a while."

Alex laughed for the first time all afternoon. "Woof, woof, Mom," she said, reaching for a roll.

Alex was astounded. Everything was baked and packed by early evening. And she hadn't even used her powers once.

Mrs. Mack volunteered to take Alex, Annie, Chris, Robyn, and Nicole to the field to drop off the boxes, while Louis and Ray finished the cleanup at the Macks' house. Alex looked in the trunk of the car before she got in. Two boxes were packed to the brim with plastic silverware and an assortment of paper plates, cups, and napkins. In another box were the decorations and various condiments for the hot food: mustard, ketchup, and pickles, along with salt, pepper, and sugar packets. And in a paper bag were aluminum foil and all sizes of garbage bags. The baked goods, including numerous pans and trays of brownies, cookies, and cupcakes, would be transported to the field Saturday morning.

It only took a short time to reach the soaring field. As the others unloaded the car, Alex and Annie volunteered to put up signs on telephone poles leading to the field. Alex had thought about taking the car with her sister, but the way her day had gone, the last thing she wanted to do was allow "lead-foot" Annie to drive her around.

"How many poles will need posters, Alex?" asked Annie, going through the box filled with signs.

"I'm guessing just four. We'll put one on the road that's perpendicular to this one, then the other three on poles leading up to the field."

"Gotcha," Annie said. She turned a sign over

and looked at it. "Louis definitely did this one."

Annie held up the sign to Alex. In bright fluorescent orange letters, it read: FIELD AWARENESS DAY—WINDSOCK FIELD. SATURDAY, 10 A.M. TO 3 P.M.

"So?" Alex said, looking up at her sister.

"Read the fine print at the bottom."

Alex scrunched up her eyes. Under the large fluorescent lettering were several small characters written in blue. It read: LOUIS DRISCOLL, TICKET TAKER EXTRAORDINAIRE. Alex rolled her eyes. "Well, at least he didn't put it in bold print."

Alex and Annie carried two signs each and walked a half mile down the dusty road to the main street. As they reached the first pole, Alex held the sign, and Annie used Mr. Mack's hammer to pound two nails into the poster board. As they walked back down the road to the airfield, Alex hardly said a word. It was a beautiful evening, and she had had enough excitement for the day. Everything seemed to be coming along perfectly.

As Annie hammered in the last poster, Alex noticed dust was being churned up down the dirt road. She strained to see and was surprised when she saw the dust settle and heard a car door slam. "Annie? Do you see anything?" she asked.

"Nope. We'd have to walk back over that small rise to see."

Alex was puzzled. Why did the car stop—and what was it doing? She jogged up the small incline and gasped. In the road was a red van. The man with the brown leather jacket and dark blue hat was ripping down a Field Day sign!

As Annie came running up, Alex grabbed her arm. "That's him, Annie!" she said, pointing to the man. "That's the guy I keep seeing everywhere!"

"What?" Annie stopped talking and realized that the man was tearing down the sign. "Hey, you! Stop!"

Alex started running toward the man, with Annie on her heels. He looked up, turned, and ran back to the van. Alex still couldn't see his face, and she knew she couldn't catch up with him, either. She stopped, and Annie slammed into her.

Alex raised her hand, ready to send out a zapper. Her only thought was to stop the man, and she knew she couldn't outrun the van. The only way to stop him was by sending out a zapper.

"No, Alex, don't! Someone might see you!" Annie yelled at her.

Alex stopped and lowered her hand, frustrated. She knew Annie was right. It was great to be able to throw electric charges from your fingertips. It was another thing to expose your powers to someone—especially someone who might be looking for the GC-161 kid. They watched as the man put the van into reverse and backed up. In his hurry, he struck the pole and something cracked. He threw the van into forward and peeled down the road.

"That was him, Annie," Alex said, as the van turned left and roared down the main road. They started walking toward the sign left in the road. "First I saw him at the mall. Then when we talked to Mr. Gordon at the soaring field. And now this. Annie, I thought he was after me. But now I'm not so sure. I'm beginning to think he's after the field," she said, looking down at the torn sign.

"I'm beginning to think you're right." Annie picked up the sign.

"But who is it? The developers?" asked Alex.

Annie shook her head. She pulled out some tape and stuck the two pieces together, then again hammered the sign on the pole. "I don't know. Maybe it was one of the pilots, mad because he had to work tomorrow. All I know is we'd better get back. I don't like being out here with that guy driving around nearby."

The two sisters walked quickly back toward the soaring field. For the first time in a long time, Alex *totally* agreed with Annie.

CHAPTER 8

Mrs. Mack beeped the horn one more time. She had already taken Annie back home to bake more brownies. Then she dropped Ray and Louis off at their houses while Alex, Nicole, and Robyn finished putting up the last of the decorations in the hangar across from the terminal.

Nicole stood by the car and yelled, "Come on, Alex! Everything's set for tomorrow. Really. Time to go home!"

Alex took a step outside the terminal door, then suddenly stopped. "Wait a minute," she said, holding up her hand. "Did I remember to call the pizza place?"

Robyn folded her arms and sighed. "Yes, for the tenth time. You called them before we came over here. They said they'd drop off the pizzas by nine-thirty tomorrow morning. Don't you remember?"

"I think I do. But did I call the right one?" she said, talking rapidly. "I mean, could I have called the one on Justin Avenue instead of Monroe Street? Is that possible?"

Nicole stepped in front of Alex. "Listen to me, Alex," she said patiently, putting her hands on Alex's shoulders. "Everything is fine. There is no problem."

"Yeah, but—"

"No buts," Nicole insisted. "Now just get into the car and—"

"Alex!" came Chris's voice from the office. "Did you remember to call Mr. Parker and ask to borrow his grill?"

Alex's eyes went wide. "Oh, gee. See, Nicole? I just knew I forgot something!"

As Alex rushed back to the office, Nicole shook her head. "Thanks, Chris," she said softly. She shrugged as she turned to Robyn and Mrs. Mack. "Well, Mrs. Mack, looks like it's just us."

Barbara Mack nodded. "That's all right. Bud Gordon said he'd take her home. I knew she wouldn't want to leave so soon. Jump in, kids. I'll get you home."

Exhausted and frazzled, Alex finally sat down on a small chair in the main terminal office. She looked at the list on her lap. Yes, she remembered to call the pizza place. Yes, she called two people and asked to borrow their gas grills for the hot dogs. And yes, she definitely asked two people to bring their boom boxes to provide the music. Happily, she crossed off the last three "to do" things on her list.

Chris and Mr. Gordon were finishing up the last-minute paperwork. She leaned back and began to think about the things she had to do in the morning. Suddenly, her tired mind switched to the man with the leather jacket and blue cap. Was he really trying to ruin Mr. Gordon's business? Chris had said the developer was dressed differently but could it be one of the developer's employees? And should she mention any of this to Mr. Gordon?

"You're doing a great job, Alex," said Mr. Gordon, breaking into her thoughts. He gathered some papers from the desk. "Especially for the short amount of time you had to get ready.

You're quite an organizer. I'd hire you to work for me any day."

Alex put her hand over her mouth as she yawned. "Thanks, Mr. Gordon. But only if you promised not to have a 'Field Awareness Day' every weekend."

Mr. Gordon laughed. "Don't you worry. Now, Chris and I have to put a few more things away and lock up."

Chris went over to her chair and gently pulled her up by the arms. "We shouldn't be long," he said, smiling. "We'll meet you at the car."

Alex smiled back, then walked outside the terminal into the cool night breeze. It was supposed to be a clear, warm day Saturday—a perfect day for soaring. The early evening was also nice, the moon shining brightly on the horizon. As Alex listened, she could hear crickets in the distance. Where she lived, a few crickets would chatter in the backyard. But in the soaring field, away from the main parts of town, they made quite a racket. *There must be hundreds of them,* she thought, *a regular chorus of singing crickets.*

Suddenly, she heard a loud thump. Then something shattering, like someone dropping a glass jar. The noises were coming from the hangar across the gravel driveway. "Hello?" she said, weakly. There was another thump. Someone was inside the hangar!

Alex tiptoed across the driveway, wincing as the gravel made crunching noises underneath her sneakers. She made her way to the side of the hangar and stood behind a small bush. Looking into the window, she saw the outlines of the many gliders and again heard a noise inside. There was only one thing to do: See who was wandering in the hangar.

And the best way to spy on the noise was to morph.

Alex looked back at the field office, and saw Chris and Mr. Gordon still busy putting papers away. She looked around, then crouched down behind the bush. Closing her eyes and concentrating, she morphed, her entire body tingling as she quickly turned into a puddle of liquid. She slithered into the hangar and along the far wall, oozing over a wrench, around two tool boxes, and under a nearby bench. She stopped at the end of the bench and looked around.

Suddenly, there was a noise to her left. Her heart beat faster as she turned her attention to the sound. Alex froze. Near the far wall, she saw two small lights. She strained to see in the dark—then she began to chuckle. There, sitting and licking its paws, was a large raccoon near a garbage can. She had seen his eyes reflecting in the moonlight.

Alex watched the animal as it continued to paw through the trash. The raccoon had already made quite a mess. In his search for food, he had pushed over a recycling bin, scattering several jars, cans, and pieces of plastic around the hangar floor. He was now tearing into a plastic garbage bag, sniffing at several fast-food wrappers and stained paper plates. He finally settled on an empty tuna can and waddled out the hangar door.

Am I ever getting jumpy, she thought. She was about to remorph when she heard another noise just outside the hangar. As she watched from under the bench, she saw a figure walking quickly by the hangar door.

It was the man who had been following her! Head down and cap over his eyes, he was heading for a red van on the other side of the hangar!

Alex remorphed in record time and raced across the hangar in the man's direction. As she reached the mess made by the raccoon, she saw a half-eaten peach right in her path. It was too late—she hit the peach pit with her foot and landed on the ground with a thud.

She brushed off her hands and looked up. The man was already traveling at a high rate of speed in the red van down the dirt road. She watched as he braked near the stop sign. Then, wheels spinning and screeching, he turned left and headed down the main road.

Chris and Mr. Gordon came running out of the office. "Alex! Are you all right? Who was that?" Chris asked breathlessly as he reached her and extended a hand.

"Yes, I'm all right. But I don't know who that was," she answered. Still slightly shaken from her fall and from remorphing so fast, she took his hand and stood up. "But he was hanging around the hangar. I may have scared him away." She turned to Chris's father. "Mr. Gordon, do you know anyone who drives a red van?"

"Not that I can think of," Mr. Gordon replied. He turned on the hangar lights and pointed to the garbage on the floor. "Did he do that?"

"No," Alex answered. "I saw a raccoon scamper out of the hangar just before the guy took off in his van."

Mr. Gordon shook his head. "What else can happen? Come on, Chris. You start cleaning up this mess. I'll help after I check the gliders, just in case our mystery man tried something. And we'd better keep the hangars closed from now on."

"Who do you think it was, Dad?"

"I really don't know. But I bet it was Ace Developers."

Alex said nothing. *Could it really be the developer?* she wondered. Or was the man after her? She wished with all her heart that she could tell Chris and his father what she feared, but she knew better. She had to keep it to herself.

CHAPTER 9

"Alex, what are you doing? I thought all the food has been ordered for tomorrow."

Alex looked up at her sister, then turned back to the phone book on her desk. "It has, I hope," she said. "I'm looking up Ace Developers."

"Trying to improve your mind and body?"

"Developers as in construction, Annie, not people," Alex said, turning a yellow page.

"I know. You're building your own mall so you can go on massive shopping sprees?"

Alex snapped her fingers. "Annie—that's it! Thank you!" She reached for the phone and punched in the number she read from the directory. She wanted to get some information about the developers, and Annie's comment had given her an idea.

Annie stood by and watched. "What are you doing? Nothing's open this late."

Alex held up her hand as someone said hello on the other end. "Yes, is this Ace Developers?" she said into the phone. "My name is Annie Mack, and I was wondering if you could help me. I'm doing a school paper on malls in Paradise Valley. And I was wondering—do you know about any land in the area that would be big enough to build a mall? . . . You know, an average size mall . . ." she added, picking up a nearby pen and scribbling something down in the margin of the phone book. "Windsock Field . . . and the old racing field near Meadow Creek? Yes, I know where they are . . . It is? Oh, this is a great help . . . Yes . . . Thanks so much. Bye." Alex set the phone down and let out a deep breath.

"You found your calling, sister," said Annie, folding her arms. "You should be a detective. But next time, don't use *my* name."

"Sorry. I panicked when he answered and that was the first thing that came to mind." Alex stared at what she had written down, then shook her head. "He did say something interesting. Windsock Field is big enough for a mall, but the old racing field is much better land. He said that they'd rather develop the racing field for a mall—and not Windsock Field."

"So why would the developers be tearing down the signs or following you around?" said Annie, trying to reason out the problem. "Did they cause all the other problems at the field, and if so, why?"

Alex threw her pen on the phone book in frustration. "My thoughts exactly, Annie. Maybe Mr. Gordon is wrong. Maybe the developers *aren't* after the field. But then, who is?"

It was finally Saturday. Louis was sitting between Alex and Ray in the Macks' car. As Louis looked out the back window, he whistled. "Ray, check out all the cars behind us!"

"Yeah. Cool, huh?"

"Who'd you ask?" Louis said.

Ray turned halfway in his seat and began pointing. "Let's see. That's Gail, from Spanish class. She's helping with the food. And that's Dave, from English class. He said he'd help carry boxes, or you know, help clean up stuff. I think Barb and Val are back there, too."

Alex was hardly listening as she kept running over the list of things to do on her lap. It had already been a long morning. Her stomach growled, reminding her that she had only had a small blueberry muffin for breakfast. She'd only had time for a muffin because it had taken her about twenty minutes to decide what to wear. The red Windsock T-shirt everyone agreed on wearing didn't seem to go with anything. She finally settled on her blue jeans—the ones without the hole in the knee.

"Annie said she invited some of her friends, too," Ray continued. "I think she even—" He stopped in midsentence as something out the window caught his eye. Alex looked in the direction of Ray's stare. As the car pulled up to the field, she could see Chris, Mr. Gordon, and Mr. Hollenbeck standing at the runway.

Or at least what was left of the runway. The grassy flat field was a mess. Clumps of sod and mud lay everywhere. Alex knew that it would be hard for the sailplanes to land on such a bumpy runway. Not only that, a big farm tractor was sitting in the middle of the field, its front tires stuck in the mud.

Everyone poured out of their cars and vans and headed for the field. Chris ran up to Alex, pointing back toward the runway. "It's a mess, Alex! Someone tore up the field with our own tractor. And we can't get the thing to start—so we can't get it out of there."

As they reached the runway, Mr. Gordon was frowning. "I'm sorry, Alex. I know how hard you've worked, but I think we're going to have to cancel today's field day."

Mr. Hollenbeck nodded sadly. "Seems so."

Alex felt sick to her stomach. It was impossible. How could someone do such a thing to the field? She looked around for a minute, pushing a chunk of sod with her foot. Desperately she asked, "Is there any way to fix this? We can't give up now."

Chris looked at her, startled. "We can't have the field day with the runway like this."

"But can't it be fixed?"

Mr. Gordon looked around. "We'd have to put the sod back in. Then shovel and rake the muddy areas so they're relatively flat. It would take a while."

"Not with all these people to help." Alex turned to the crowd around her. She was determined not to let anything spoil the field day. Everyone had worked so hard. No one—not even the man in the dark blue cap—was going to make the soaring field look bad. Not while she was in charge. "All right, everyone. You heard Mr. Gordon. Let's start putting back the sod. Do you have any rakes and shovels, Mr. Gordon?"

"Plenty. In the storage shed," he said, pulling out several keys from his pocket. "I'll open the shed. Those of you who want to rake or shovel, come with me."

Mr. Hollenbeck climbed on the tall tractor and tried to start the motor. It whirred once, then fell silent. Alex walked over to the tractor and shook her head at Mr. Hollenbeck.

"We can't even push it," he said, trying the key again. It clicked in protest.

"What happened to it?" she asked.

"Whoever left it here also left the lights on. Drained the batteries completely." Mr. Hollenbeck pointed to a black box on the side of the tractor. "And if you look at the battery, the charge light isn't even lit."

"Maybe we can push it," Alex suggested.

"It will take several of us," Mr. Hollenbeck said. "I'll go grab a few people."

As Mr. Hollenbeck ran back to the crowd at the storage shed, Alex looked around. Mr. Gordon was handing out the tools, so everyone was busy talking, raking, or shoveling. No one was paying any attention to the tractor—or to her. They had to get the tractor out of there, and she knew the best way to do it.

She moved to the other side of the vehicle, placing herself between the tractor and the others. Concentrating hard, she pointed her finger and zapped the dead battery. The battery seemed to spark as the motor protested. She heard a loud *poof,* then it rumbled to a start.

The motor was running, but the tractor was still not moving. Using her telekinetic powers, she began to push the machine. It was difficult to move because the front wheels were stuck in the mud, especially the right wheel. She concentrated even harder. The tractor rocked a little, then started to move forward—very slowly at first, then faster.

"Chris! Mr. Gordon!" she yelled, running from behind the vehicle. "The tractor!"

Several people swarmed toward the tractor, catching up with the moving machine. Mr. Gordon jumped on the seat and pulled on the brake. He looked down at Alex with a surprised expression on his face. "Now, how did that happen?"

"It just started rolling," Alex yelled above the loud motor.

He nodded, then shrugged. "I'll take it back to the storage shed where it belongs!" he yelled. "You go help the others!"

As Alex walked back to help rake, she wondered who would want to wreck the field. Not only that, Mr. Gordon had said the tractor belonged in the storage shed—and he had just used the keys to get in the shed to grab the rakes. Did that mean whoever drove out the tractor had keys to the shed?

Alex looked back at Mr. Gordon and frowned. Who else but someone who worked with him could get hold of the keys? Was this an inside job?

CHAPTER 10

Alex couldn't believe her eyes. The line at the glider field gate was at least twenty cars long.

"How's it going?" she asked Annie, who was handing out a ticket to a man in a nearby car.

Annie counted out three dollars in change and handed it through the window. "Thanks, sir . . . Great, if you don't count the time I shortchanged a guy three bucks," Annie answered, adjusting her Windsock Field cap.

Alex knew how she felt. She was on a break,

but she had been working in the food tent for about two hours straight, and the lines had been long since the time they opened for business. Just after they opened, Alex accidentally gave a woman a five dollar bill in change instead of a one dollar bill. The woman had been nice enough to correct Alex, who vowed to be more careful with the money.

She watched her sister hand out another ticket. "Need more help? I could get Nicole—"

"Nope. Mom went to get some more change. She said she'd help when she got back. Probably in about ten minutes."

Alex backed away as her sister continued to work. "Catch you later." She wandered back to the food tent set up near the main terminal, smiling contentedly all the way. They had finally smoothed out the runway so the gliders could take off. Mr. Gordon had even commented that the grass was better than before. They had only been about fifteen minutes behind schedule when they let the first cars through the gate. And two hours later, it seemed as if everything were running along perfectly. No problems—and no man in a dark blue cap.

When she reached the food tent, Alex found

Robyn, Nicole, Ray, and several of the other kids from school working at top speed, handing out brownies, cookies, bags of chips, pizza, hot dogs, and drinks. Every now and then, Robyn would resupply the balloon bunches spread around the tent, making sure any child that walked by had a red or white balloon with the Windsock Field logo on the front.

The soaring field was busy, too. About every fifteen minutes, a tow plane and its trailing glider would take off from the runway and another glider would land.

Alex looked over at the terminal's covered porch and waved to Louis. His line—to get tickets for the soaring rides—was long, too. "Come and get it!" he was saying. "Yes, indeed-ie, folks, take a ride in a glider. It's fun. It's stupendous. It's tremendous. Step right up."

As he continued his speech, he began to look around as if he had lost something. Alex walked behind the ticket table and asked, "Need something, Louis?"

"Alex! You little lifesaver. Yes, I need some more tickets," he said, holding up an empty roll of tickets.

"Where—"

"I'll get them. You just woman the fort and do what I do: Tell all these lovely people what a joy it is to go on a glider."

"But, Louis, you've never been on a glider. How can you—" she answered, whispering.

"I lived vicariously through all of you the other day," he said dramatically. "And besides, you'd be surprised at what I know. " He wiggled his eyebrows and slipped by Alex.

Alex looked out at about twenty waiting faces in line. "Yes . . . Well . . . I guess I can tell you all . . . gliding really is fun," she said. She cleared her throat and tried not to get too nervous. "Um . . . Louis is getting more tickets."

"Have you been in a glider, honey?" asked an older woman in the back.

"Yes. About a week ago. It was great. When you get up there, all you hear is the wind rushing past the glider. Everyone looks like ants, and the houses look like those pieces in the Monopoly game. And you're up so high—"

Louis pushed his way by Alex, a roll of tickets in his hand. "Thank you, ladies and gentlemen. You've been very patient. Now, who's next to enjoy the ride of a lifetime?" He leaned over to Alex. "We're A-OK now, Alex. I can handle it from here. Oh, by the way, the office door was wide-open. Some guy was wandering around nearby, so I closed it."

Alex nodded at Louis, then turned to walk back to the food tent. She stopped halfway. *Uh, oh,* she thought, *Some guy? What guy? Maybe he was trying to find something in the office! Or destroy something!* Staring into the crowd, she tried to spot Chris, Mr. Gordon, or Mr. Hollenbeck. She finally saw Mr. Hollenbeck standing near a post at the food tent, taking a break and drinking a soda.

"Mr. Hollenbeck!" she shouted, running up to him.

He turned to her and smiled. "Alex. Hey, everything is going great."

"Yes, it's great," she replied, not quite as enthusiastically. She scanned the crowd, then turned to him. "Is the terminal office supposed to be open?"

Mr. Hollenbeck took a gulp of his soda and shook his head. "No, of course not. Why?"

"Louis was getting more tickets from the office a minute ago. He said the door was wide-open, so he closed it."

"Good. Good," he said, looking out at a glider

landing on the field. "Then there's no problem, right?"

"But—"

He threw his unfinished drink into the garbage. "Well, I have to go back to work. You, too, young lady."

Alex watched as Mr. Hollenbeck walked back to the glider field. Puzzled, she turned back to the food tent.

Ray looked up and smiled at his friend. "Watcha thinking about?" he said, wiping his hands on his apron. "Something wrong?"

Alex frowned and shook her head. "I don't know. Maybe just a bit weird."

"If you want weird, just come back here and work again." He leaned toward Alex and pointed to a boy standing near the garbage can. "See that little kid over there? He's had four hot dogs in less than an hour."

"Four? Where are his parents?"

Ray nodded to the right. "Over there. They've had three each themselves. I think they're in hot dog heaven."

Alex laughed as she slipped around the concession table. Maybe she was overreacting to every little thing. Maybe Mr. Gordon just forgot to close the office door. And maybe the guy was just walking by the office on his way to the rest room. Alex soon stopped worrying as she handed out pizzas and carefully counted out change, all the while explaining the thrills and chills of soaring to whomever asked.

An hour later, the crowd seemed to thin out. Chris wandered over to the food tent and examined the tin of brownies sitting on the concession table. "Gee, Robyn. Could you cut the brownies any smaller?" he joked, pointing to the tray.

"That's our fourth tin," Robyn said, crossing her arms. "We only made seven, so we're being conservative. Right, Nicole?"

"As always," said Nicole, running after a plastic cup blowing by. Throwing it into a recycling container, she said, "Why do people just drop their plastic cups? I should have made up a sign to recycle them in this bin."

Alex pulled a marker from her pocket. "Find me some paper and we'll write one up," she said, popping off the cap. Nicole dragged out a large box from under the table and ripped off a side of the box to use as a sign.

"*Voilà!* That should do it," Nicole said, handing the cardboard to Alex.

Chris leaned over the table and watched as Alex drew the letters on the cardboard. "Everything's going great, Alex," he said, smiling at her.

Alex took off her cap and ran her hand through her bangs. "Thanks, Chris. I just hope we impress the inspectors when they get here. They'll really be surprised to see this many people."

"They're already here," he said, chuckling at Alex's surprised look. "There's one over there, standing by the picnic tables near Lenny and Whitey, our two mechanics." Alex turned to see the two men in blue overalls talking to a man in white shorts and a red top.

"That inspector's talking to people who just came off the rides," Chris said. "There's another guy over by the ticket sales booth—that man in the white T-shirt and jeans. He's listening to the comments made by the people in line."

"Are you kidding me? Why didn't you tell us?" asked Robyn, suddenly straightening everything on the table.

"Don't worry, Robyn. You're all doing fine," Chris said, reaching for a brownie. "I can tell they like everything by the way they keep nodding and smiling. How much is the brownie, Ray?"

"A quarter. But for you, ten dollars," he said, putting out his hand.

"Wrong again. Here's a quarter."

Ray shrugged and dropped the coin in the cash box. "And what if the inspectors see something wrong?"

"They can cancel the accreditation application. And if that happens, the land will definitely go to Ace Developers," Chris said, his face turning grim.

"But that won't happen, right?" Alex said, looking around at her friends. Everyone nodded in reply.

Alex and Chris watched as Mr. Gordon's glider was towed into the sky with the tow plane. Right on cue, the glider dropped the towline, seemed to rock back and forth, then leveled off. "And the best thing?" Chris said, pointing with his thumb. "Dad's just gone up with one of the inspectors, Mr. Stewart—a real nice guy. I think he's impressed with the school."

"All right! Was he the guy who asked for the soda from you, Ray?" asked Robyn.

"Yeah, he said his name," replied Ray, "as if

I were supposed to know him. Maybe you should have asked him to wear a name tag that read, 'Mr. Stewart, Inspector.' That way we would have given him the soda for free—you know, really impress him."

"I don't think an inspector could be bribed with a soda, Ray," said Nicole, cutting a fresh batch of brownies. "Now, brownies, maybe. Especially since I made them."

Alex looked back at Chris. "Oh, I know what I was going to ask you. Is the office door supposed to be—"

Alex never finished her sentence. Chris was looking up with an alarmed expression on his face. "That's funny," he said to no one in particular. "Who's that coming in?" He made a choking noise, then dropped his brownie on the table. "It's my dad's plane!" he suddenly shouted.

"What?" Alex said, trying to block out the sun with one hand. She searched the sky for Mr. Gordon's glider.

Chris hesitated for a second and pointed in the direction of the glider. "It's coming in for a landing early—and it's banking too far to the right," he said. He turned and ran at full speed toward a nearby Windsock van. "Whitey! Lenny! I need the rescue van! Quick! It's Dad!"

The two men sitting at a nearby picnic table looked up. In less than a second, they dropped their hot dogs and took off for the rescue van—with Alex right on their heels.

CHAPTER 11

The man named Lenny jumped into the driver's side of the van as Chris and Whitey climbed in the back. Alex pulled at the back door, not allowing it to close.

"Chris," she said, breathlessly, "do you know what's wrong with the plane?"

"Looks like his left aileron is flapping. It's making him turn that way," Chris said.

"Aileron? What's that?" she asked.

"A small wingletlike part of the wing. It's on the back of the wing and it's only supposed to move by the inside controls. It's not very big, but it's big enough to cause a problem."

"So that little part of the left back wing shouldn't flop like that?" Alex asked, shielding her eyes with her hand and staring at the ailing glider.

"That's right. Looks like maybe the linkage is broken. It may have corroded. Either way, it's going to be a tricky landing," Chris said as Lenny started up the van.

Alex stepped back as the van sped off down the field. She looked up at the glider and squinted. *Please don't crash. Please be safe,* she thought, shuddering. The plane was low enough for her to make out the flapping aileron, and it definitely looked wrong.

Ray came running in Alex's direction. "Alex! What's happened?" he asked, catching up to her.

She pointed to the glider as it continued to lean to one side. "That glider's back winglet isn't supposed to flap like that. Ray, how far do you think my telekinetic powers go?" she whispered frantically.

"I don't know. You moved something a few backyards away once, remember?"

"Yeah, but this is at least a few hundred feet in the air," she said, still staring at the glider. "Well, I can't just stand here and talk about it. I have to do something."

"But what can you do?" Ray said, looking at his friend.

"That part of the wing that's flapping has to be flat. If I can keep it flat, except when I feel the pressure from the controls, then maybe . . ." She looked around. No one was watching, and only Ray was standing nearby. She hesitated, trying to gather her strength. "Well . . . here goes."

Alex stared hard at the glider's flapping winglet, concentrating all her telekinetic power on the moving aileron. As she watched, the aileron started to move to a flat position, then flopped back down. *Oh, no,* she thought, *it's too far away. It's not working!*

"Come on, Alex, concentrate," Ray encouraged. "I know you can do it."

Alex focused even harder. Slowly, the aileron moved into a flat position. The glider righted itself and was no longer leaning to the right. Alex kept up her concentration as the plane came closer to the runway and leveled off for the landing position.

Suddenly the bright sun was in her eyes. "I lost it, Ray!" she said, trying to keep her voice down. The plane disappeared in the sunlight only for a moment, but it was enough to make Alex's heart pound fast. When she could see the glider again, it was beginning to wobble slightly. She concentrated again and the aileron seemed to stabilize. She felt a tug on the winglet and realized Mr. Gordon was working the controls. When she felt the slight tugs, she let the aileron move, and gradually the plane came lower toward the field. Finally, for what seemed to Alex like hours—but was only minutes—the glider's wheel gently touched down on the grassy runway.

"Way to go, Alex," Ray enthusiastically whispered to his friend, putting his arm around her shoulders and giving her a quick hug. Alex smiled weakly.

Everyone seemed to be running toward the glider from everywhere. The rescue van was there first, and in the distance, Alex could see Chris and his dad embrace. Some of the public were also wandering on the field, trying to see what the excitement was about—many believing it was part of the field day activities.

Alex and Ray ran to the field toward the glider. As they arrived at the plane, the inspector, white and shaken, was just being helped out of the plane by Mr. Gordon.

Chris looked at his father. "What happened, Dad?"

Mr. Gordon shook his head. "We were coming out of the tow, and suddenly the plane leaned to the left. I knew it was the aileron. But no matter what movement I made, I couldn't correct the problem. When we were coming back in, it seemed to correct itself. Maybe the winds caught it and held it there. Maybe it just got stuck at the right time."

Alex and Ray exchanged quick glances.

"Either way, we managed to land all right," Mr. Gordon turned to Lenny. "See anything, Lenny?"

Lenny dug his finger in between the wing and the aileron. "Yup. Looks like you have a loose linkage all right. The screw's loose—just enough to cause a problem."

The inspector harumphed. "Don't you usually inspect your glider before each flight, Mr. Gordon?"

Mr. Gordon turned to the inspector. "Yes, Mr. Stewart, I do," he said, a twinge of resentment in his voice. "I inspected this one, too. And it's my best glider."

"But yet, the screw is loose?" Mr. Stewart raised an eyebrow.

"Mr. Stewart," said Chris's father, standing up

straighter, "we run a tight ship around here, sir. Things like this just don't happen."

Mr. Stewart harumphed again. "I hope not, for your sake, Mr. Gordon."

"Really, we—"

The inspector held up his hand. "That's enough, Mr. Gordon. I have to speak with the other inspectors now. Excuse me." Mr. Stewart leaned over into the glider and picked up his clipboard. He turned and nodded to Mr. Gordon, then continued on his way to find the other inspectors.

Alex looked at Ray. "I can't believe Mr. Gordon would make a mistake. He always checks his planes before he goes up." She shook her head. "Ray, are you thinking what I'm thinking?"

Ray nodded. "Mister leather jacket and blue cap is responsible. But when would he have had a chance to tamper with the glider?"

Alex looked at Chris's dad. "Mr. Gordon? You know, there has been a suspicious-looking guy around here in the past week. I think I may know who . . . well, not really who . . . I just keep seeing the same guy around all the time."

"What does he look like, Alex?" asked Mr. Gordon, walking over to stand next to her.

"He always wears a brown leather jacket, even when it's hot. And a dark blue hat that reads USS *Ohio*— with a gold braid."

"Ohio?" Mr. Gordon muttered.

Alex nodded. "First I saw him when Chris and I went to the mall. Then I saw him here three more times," she explained. "Once the first day I flew in a glider, then when Annie and I were hanging up signs, and again last night just before you took me home."

"Why didn't you say something, Alex?" asked Chris, putting his hands on his hips.

Alex hesitated. How could she tell them that she originally thought the man was after her? She couldn't do that without exposing her powers from the GC-161.

"I guess I really thought it was a coincidence—until last night," she said, which was somewhat true. "And now, with the loose screw. Well, if someone did fool with the linkage—"

"But, Alex—" Chris started to say.

"Chris," Mr. Gordon interrupted. "I can see Alex's point. I probably wouldn't have suspected anything, either. And she doesn't know who works here and who doesn't. Don't be mad at her."

Alex let out a sigh of relief. She was grateful

to Mr. Gordon. After all, they all could have asked Alex some very tough questions—especially if she mentioned that she thought the man was following *her*.

"We'll deal with this later. Let's all get back to work," said Mr. Gordon, moving to the back of the glider. "Chris? Help me push the glider back to the hangar. In the meantime, Lenny? Whitey? Make sure everyone checks their gliders before each takeoff—and check the grounds to make sure everything is secure."

Chris moved to the side of the glider to help his father. He looked at Alex and smiled sheepishly. "Sorry, Alex, if I was kind of hard on you. It was my dad up there."

Alex walked over and patted his shoulder, then nodded. "I know, Chris. I would have felt the same way."

As the crowd dispersed and Mr. Gordon and Chris pushed the glider toward the hangar, Alex looked toward the main building. There stood the three inspectors, talking among themselves. Occasionally, one would point to something on the field or to a hangar—or nod toward Mr. Gordon. She wondered what they were talking about and how she could prove to them that the near-accident was probably not Mr. Gordon's fault.

But she had no way to prove that someone had fooled with the sailplane. To the inspectors, it looked as if Mr. Gordon had not done a safety inspection on his glider before he took off. Alex couldn't believe that—and she wouldn't believe it. She knew Chris's father was just too careful.

Suddenly, Alex grabbed Ray's arm. "Ray, look!"

Sitting in the parking lot near the food tent was a red van.

"Come on, Alex. If you've seen one red van, you've seen them all," said Ray, walking slowly back to the food tent.

"No, Ray," she said, pulling her friend along. "Last night, when Annie and I were putting up signs, someone backed that van into a pole, trying to get away from us. And the driver tore down our poster. Come on!" She sprinted off toward the parking lot.

Ray scratched his head, then ran after Alex. As they reached the back of the van, Alex pointed and smiled. "Look, Ray. The left taillight is broken."

"And what does that prove, Sherlock?"

Alex frowned at him. "Don't you see? Annie

and I saw him hit the pole, and I know it was the left side. So he's here somewhere, Ray. And maybe he was the one who messed up Mr. Gordon's glider."

"It should be simple to find him. Any nut case who'd wear a leather jacket and hat in this weather will stand right out."

"Right. So come on. Let's look around." Ray followed, turning as he scanned the area. Alex stopped and looked at her friend. "Why are you spinning around like that?"

"I saw a Clint Eastwood movie once. He told some guy always keep your back to the wall. There's no wall, so I'm spinning."

"Ray, I don't think this guy is going to jump you in this crowd." She turned and started walking up the gravel drive toward the red storage shed. "Come on. We'll start up there."

As they walked toward the last hangar, Louis came running up. "Hey, guys!" he said. "What's happening? I got a break and I saw you guys up here, so I thought I'd find out what you were doing. Want some of my brownie?" He held out a piece of brownie to Alex. She shook her head and made a face. Louis took a bite and swallowed. "So what are you guys doing out here?"

Alex looked at Ray and winced. She really

didn't have the time to update Louis on all the crazy things that were happening. "Ummm . . . we were just looking for—"

She never finished her sentence. "Hey!" Louis interrupted, pointing over Alex's shoulder. "There's the guy I saw earlier—the one in the terminal near the office! He looks like he's running away from us!"

CHAPTER 12

Alex looked in the direction of Louis's pointing finger. Someone *was* running toward the red storage shed building.

"That's him. I know it is!" Louis continued. "I kept asking myself, why would anyone be wearing a leather jacket and baseball cap in this weather?"

Louis took off for the man, with Alex and Ray following close behind. As Alex watched the running man, she knew, too, that he was the same guy who kept popping up wherever she went—and the one who could have sabotaged the plane. Alex suddenly stopped as they ran past the back hangar, grabbing Louis and Ray. "Louis," she said, trying to talk between breaths. "You . . . you go get Mr. Gordon. Or Mr. Hollenbeck. Tell them to come up here right away. Okay?"

"Will you two be okay?"

Alex nodded. As Louis ran the opposite way, Ray looked at his friend. "Why did you do that?"

"This guy runs fast, and we're too far away to catch up to him, Ray," she explained. "But I think I know how to stop him." As the man ran past the storage shed, Alex held up her hand. "Is anyone watching? I have to zap the lock first."

Ray looked around quickly. Louis was out of sight and no one else was around. "The coast is clear, Al. Zap away!"

Alex closed one eye, aiming toward the storage shed door—and zapped the lock. As sparks flew, the wooden door flew open, exposing the tractor and several rakes and shovels. Alex concentrated even harder. Using her telekinetic powers, she dragged one of the rakes out of the shed. It slithered quickly through the grass like a long snake—and into the running man's path.

"Hey, you! Stop!" Ray yelled, just as the man came close to the rake.

The man started to turn his head—then stepped on the rake.

Thwap!

The handle flew up and bopped the running man in the nose, stopping him cold. He stood there for a moment, then slowly fell flat on the ground. As Alex and Ray ran toward him, he sat up. He started to rock back and forth, while holding his nose with both hands. "My nobe . . . I tink I boke my nobe," he said over and over.

Alex moved the rake out of the way, then bent down and peered under the brim of his cap. "You okay, mister?"

The man kept his hands over his nose—so she still couldn't see his face. "My nobe. My nobe. D'you hab a tissue?"

Alex pulled a tissue from her pocket and held it out to the man. Just as she did, Chris was suddenly at her side, puffing from running. Mr. Gordon was not far behind, and as he ran up to Alex, he looked at the figure sitting on the ground.

"What on earth are you doing here?" Mr. Gordon said, leaning over and panting heavily.

The man on the ground just shrugged. Mr. Gordon reached over and grabbed the dark USS *Ohio* cap off the man's head.

Alex stood back, startled. "Mr. Hollenbeck? It was *you* all this time?" she asked.

Mr. Hollenbeck shook out the tissue. He wiped his sore nose and looked up at Alex. "What are you talking about?" he said. Suddenly, everyone was asking questions all at once. Alex winced at the voices as everyone was trying to be heard.

"All right," Mr. Gordon yelled, and the voices abruptly stopped. "One at a time. Alex? You first."

Alex squatted down next to Mr. Hollenbeck, who was still holding his nose. "I kept seeing you wherever I went," she said. "Who were you following?"

"No one."

"So why were you going around wearing a leather jacket and cap in this heat?" she asked.

"I was just trying to, well . . . make everyone nervous. Cover up who I was. You know, create a few distractions," Mr. Hollenbeck said, wiping his nose again.

"Distractions?" asked Chris, his voice betraying his anger. "Your distractions may have killed my father! Or caused us to lose the soaring school!"

Mr. Gordon held up his hand. "Let's hear him out, Chris."

Mr. Hollenbeck continued. "Yeah, I guess the things I did may have harmed somebody, or the soaring school."

Chris seemed to growl. He shook his head in disgust and clenched his fists.

"I have a question, too," Louis interrupted. He cleared his throat as Mr. Hollenbeck looked at him. "Mr. Hollenbeck, why were you sneaking around the office hangar earlier? Hummm?" he said, his voice suddenly sounding like a lawyer, with Mr. Hollenbeck on trial.

"And tearing down signs for the field day yesterday?" added Alex.

Mr. Hollenbeck looked surprised, then shook his head. "No, no, no. I wasn't in the office hangar earlier. And I didn't tear down any signs. It wasn't me. It was probably Travis. Hey, Travis—over here! Meet the folks." Mr. Hollenbeck waved to someone peeking out from behind the storage shed.

Alex gasped. Walking toward the group was another man—complete with brown leather jacket and a dark blue cap with yellow trim!

"What's going on, Mr. Hollenbeck?" asked the tall man. He took off the cap and jacket. Alex thought he had to be extremely hot in the outfit. Even Mr. Hollenbeck, still in his jacket, was sweating profusely.

"Meet Travis, my duplicate," Mr. Hollenbeck said, standing up and continuing to wipe his nose. He turned to Mr. Gordon. "I admit it, I was trying to make trouble for you, Bud. I couldn't be everywhere at all times, so I got one of my buddies to help me. He's about my height and weight, so he looks the same in a leather jacket and cap. Plus, he has a red van nobody's ever seen around here before."

"The cap," said Mr. Gordon, putting his hand on his forehead. "I should have realized who you were when Alex told me about the cap with the USS *Ohio* on the front. That was your ship." Mr. Hollenbeck nodded. "But what are you after, Sam? Why are you trying to destroy the school?" Mr. Gordon's brown eyes bore into Sam.

Something was gnawing at the back of Alex's mind. She suddenly snapped her fingers. Maybe she did know what was going on. "Mr. Gordon, Chris said all the weird things started happening at the field at the end of last semester. That's about a month ago, right?"

"Yes . . ."

"And you said you cut salaries about a month

ago, so you could afford to keep the school open to have time to get accreditation." Mr. Gordon nodded. "And when did the developers last visit Windsock Field?"

"About a month ago," said Chris, wide-eyed.

Alex looked at Chris, then back to Mr. Gordon. "All this time, you thought it was Ace Developers who were causing all the trouble. But I called Ace Developers, Mr. Gordon. They're losing interest in Windsock Field as a site for the mall. They're looking at some field near Meadow Creek now."

Mr. Gordon ran his hand through his short hair and glared at his pilot. "So that was it. You were trying to make the soaring school fail before the developers lost interest, weren't you?"

Mr. Hollenbeck nodded slowly. "Sure, I'll admit it. The sprinkler system . . . the missing papers . . . the tractor . . . the glider. It was to make the soaring school look bad so the inspectors would refuse the accreditation. The developers will only wait for so long. And just think of all that money. You said if you ever had to sell the school, you'd pay your pilots the back wages you owe us. Well, this was my chance to get paid off."

"But how did you rig the glider?" asked Chris, trying to hold back his anger.

"I helped your dad and the inspector enter the glider. I was the wing-runner, remember? I took over for you," Hollenbeck said.

"That's why you told me to go take a break?" Chris took a step toward Hollenbeck, and Mr. Gordon put a restraining hand on Chris's shoulder.

Mr. Hollenbeck continued. "Yeah. I twisted the screw on the linkage just enough so it would go slack. I guess I loosened it a bit too much. But I knew Bud was a good pilot. A loose aileron wouldn't hurt him. Bud could handle it, but it would look bad in front of the inspector."

Mr. Gordon shook his head, apparently finding it difficult to believe his trusted pilot could betray him. Alex knew how he felt. She could hardly believe it, either.

"Come on, Bud," Mr. Hollenbeck continued. "Forget the school. You and I both know a mall is a much better idea. Just think of all the money you'd get for selling the place."

Mr. Gordon hesitated. "Sam, you've always been my right hand man. I can't pretend I understand why you did this. And for your sake, I'm not pressing charges. All I ask is that you leave the field—and never come back."

Mr. Hollenbeck wiped his nose again. "You don't have to ask me twice. But I still think you're making a big mistake."

As Mr. Hollenbeck and Travis walked toward the red van, Alex looked at Mr. Gordon. He seemed to age right before her eyes as he watched his one-time good friend drive away.

"Dad, what do we do about the inspectors?" Chris asked quietly. Though the mystery had been solved, Alex knew the future of the soaring school was still in jeopardy.

"And after we all explained to the inspectors what happened, they said they knew that it wasn't Mr. Gordon's fault. They'd seen that he did check his plane before he took off," Alex said. "And they were impressed with how many people were interested in the school. Oh, and they also said they liked how Mr. Gordon was so committed to keeping the school going, even with the pressure from the developers."

Annie sat on the picnic table and picked up a round pickle. "And so . . . ," Annie said, waiting expectantly to hear the final outcome.

"And so," Alex said deliberately, "they

granted Mr. Gordon his accreditation. The field can now ask for grants to keep it going."

Everyone—Annie, Mr. and Mrs. Mack, Robyn and Nicole—all cheered and applauded at the good news. Ray let out an ear-splitting whistle. Chris laughed at them all.

It was late afternoon, and the field day had been a complete success. Almost everyone had gone home—including the now satisfied inspectors—and Alex's family and friends were finally eating a well-deserved dinner.

"Why, Alex, that's wonderful," said Mrs. Mack, finishing up her turkey sandwich. "Looks like you kids did a wonderful job helping Mr. Gordon and his school."

Alex sighed and scooped out a handful of potato chips from a nearby bowl. "Yeah. We made tons of money at the food tent."

"And we made quite a bit from all the rides—except for that ride you took with my dad for free," Chris added, smiling and nudging Alex with his elbow.

Alex gave him a friendly slap on the arm. "He said it was okay!"

"Just picking on you."

"Oops," said Annie. "Speaking of rides,

where's Louis? Your dad was looking for him a while ago, Chris."

"Yeah," added Mr. Mack, leaning over the table for a brownie. "Just where is Louis? He was supposed to help me carry some of the boxes to the car."

"I don't know, Dad," replied Alex, looking around.

"Probably cleaning up the crumbs off the floor of the food tent, hoping to find a leftover cookie," added Ray.

"You should talk," replied Robyn.

"He's a growing boy, Ray," said Mrs. Mack, standing up. She lugged several garbage bags filled with recyclables and tossed them into the backseat of the car.

"Think any kids will fit in the back, Barbara?" asked Mr. Mack, staring into the backseat.

Mrs. Mack looked over his shoulder. "We could tie them to the hood."

"Mom, you wouldn't—" Alex said.

"Alex, look!" Chris interrupted, pointing to the runway. A shiny yellow glider was landing gently. As Alex watched, she saw a beaming face staring out the bubble canopy of the glider. Then the person waved frantically.

"I don't believe it," Alex muttered, breaking

into a run. Ray stammered, Chris laughed, then they both ran after Alex.

Mr. Gordon got out of the glider and helped Louis unbuckle his seat belt. "Good job, my good man," Louis was saying. He whipped out a dollar bill. "A tip for you. Keep the change."

Mr. Gordon looked puzzled for a moment, then started to laugh. "Louis, you can fly in my glider any day—just name the time, and I'll be there."

Alex, Ray, and Chris came running up. "I don't believe it," said Alex.

"This guy is great," said Mr. Gordon, putting his arm around Louis's shoulder. "He had me in stitches the entire time we were up there."

"He wasn't green?" asked Ray, incredulously.

"Nope. As a matter of fact, I think he'd make a great pilot," Mr. Gordon said.

"I guess I should confess, eh, Mr. Gordon?" As Mr. Gordon nodded, Louis turned to Alex, Ray, and Chris. "I . . . I was afraid to fly when we first started talking about going on a glider. So I met a guy named Lenny up here when we first came to the field. You know, when I disappeared on you? He said he'd take me up in his airplane so I could get used to flying. And he promised he wouldn't tell anyone. So all week, he's been taking me up in his plane after school, so I could get over my fear." He beamed broadly at Mr. Gordon. "I guess it worked, right?"

Mr. Gordon laughed again. "I can tell you were born to fly, Louis."

Alex smiled at her friend. Now wouldn't *that* be some power. *But then again,* she thought, *I think I'll just stick to zapping and morphing. That's enough excitement for me.*

About the Author

Patricia Barnes-Svarney has as many stuffed animals as Alex Mack has hats—and she's proud of it. She writes not only fiction, but nonfiction, and you can often see her name lurking in science magazine articles and along the bindings of science books for young readers and adults. When she's not writing, she likes to spend her time reading, birding, herb gardening, and hiking. She is the author of *Star Trek: The Next Generation: Starfleet Academy: Loyalties,* and *The Secret World of Alex Mack: Junkyard Jitters!* She is working on another *Star Trek* story and a nonfiction book. She lives with her husband in Endwell, New York.